"What About You, Holly?

"Have you started ~~a wish list for~~ _____ k asked, brushing h

"Yes," she half c _____ with you, Nick. T _____ you've talked abo _____

"Then I hope you're crazy about Yule logs and miniature wheat fields on windowsills." He pulled a tendril of hair from beneath her hat and wrapped it around his finger.

His mood had shifted. He was smiling—a magical, mystical smile. The moment was made more magical by the scent of pine, the feel of his strong arms.

"Did I mention the lighting of the first fire? Or the drawing of the first water? I promise you, it's not for the weak of heart."

Weak of heart? His final words stirred something in her, a knowing from within so intense she felt a need to step back out of his arms.

"There's nothing weak about the way I feel about you, Nick," Holly said quietly.

Dear Reader:

Happy Holidays to all of you!

This December brings not only three sensational books by familiar favorites—Jennifer Greene, Annette Broadrick and Sara Chance—but wonderful stories from a couple of newcomers: Jackie Merritt and Terry Lawrence. There's also a fabulous Christmas bonus, *'Tis the Season* by Noreen Brownlie, a novel full of the Christmas spirit about the best gift of all—the gift of love.

January marks the beginning of a very special new year, a twelve-month extravaganza with Silhouette Desire. We've declared 1989 the Year of the Man, and we're spotlighting one book each month as a tribute to the Silhouette Desire hero—our Man of the Month!

Created by your favorite authors, you'll find these men utterly irresistible. You'll be swept away by Diana Palmer's Mr. Janaury, (whom some might remember from a brief appearance in *Fit for a King*), and Joan Hohl's Mr. February is every woman's idea of the perfect Valentine....

Don't let these men get away!

Yours,

Isabel Swift
Senior Editor & Editorial Coordinator

NOREEN BROWNLIE
'Tis the Season

Silhouette Desire

Published by Silhouette Books New York

America's Publisher of Contemporary Romance

SILHOUETTE BOOKS
300 East 42nd St., New York, N.Y. 10017

ISBN: 0-373-05468-8

First Silhouette Books printing December 1988

Printed in the U.S.A.

NOREEN BROWNLIE

grew up in a large family on the Oregon coast, surrounded by Victorian houses, fishing boats and romantic sunsets. She met her husband while she was working inland as a television writer/producer, and the couple recently resettled in Seattle, where he continues to work in broadcasting and Noreen lives her dream of writing fiction full-time. There are always animals and close family ties in her romances—subjects dear to her heart. Noreen has also written as Jamisan Whitney.

With love to my husband
J.C.
my companion along The Way

Prologue

I have a confession to make."

The deep male voice was familiar. Captured by the word *confession*, Holly Peterson looked up from chopping celery to stare at her television screen. The voice belonged to a distinguished senior anchorman at one of Portland's top-rated stations.

"As a broadcaster," he continued, "I see a lot of stories about heroism, unselfish acts and volunteer work, and I find myself asking why haven't *I* done more to help others?" He brought a hand to his chest as he delivered the rhetorical question.

Holly's attention wavered from the public service spot as she sliced through the remaining celery on her cutting board, but her inner voice couldn't be ignored. It confronted her with the same niggling question, and she looked up again.

"This year I decided to take action and do something, to give a part of myself to others." As the camera pulled back, the aging newsman was seen standing in front of a brightly lit Christmas tree. A cozy fireplace blazed in the background. "I decided to become a link in the Chain of Caring."

Holly set her cleaver down and leaned closer to the television set on her kitchen counter. It was late October, and though the Christmas tree looked strangely out of place, the scene tugged at her. Why? As a cosmetologist, she was used to the artificial world created by sets, makeup, costumes and lighting. She'd watched actors deliver lines dozens of times. But for some inexplicable reason this message touched her as a person, not a professional.

The popular broadcaster sat down on a sofa beside a white-haired woman. "This is Alice," he said softly, taking a frail hand in his. "I've committed myself to helping her with errands and chores through the winter months." As he described the plight of many of Portland's elderly shut-ins, the older woman's eyes glistened.

Holly felt tears spring to her own eyes. The tree, the fire, the white-haired woman—they were all reminders her mother was gone. This would be Holly's first Christmas without a single family member.

A phone number appeared on the lower third of the screen, but her hands were too wet to grab pen and paper. Quickly she took handfuls of celery slices and made small piles to represent the digits.

The male voice continued. "I encourage you to call the number on your screen and help make the coming holiday season brighter for someone in need. Or, if you're elderly and want help or companionship during the winter months, call to register with the Volunteer Bureau, as well.''

Holly glanced at the clock. The salad she was making for her lunch could wait. Besides, it was going to be a slow day at the salon. After drying her hands, she reached for the phone and counted out each pile of celery to dial the number. A recording informed her all lines were tied up and asked her to wait for a volunteer coordinator.

As she shifted from one foot to the other, Holly brooded over her impulsive action. The public service announcement had certainly pushed all of her buttons. The thought of brightening the holidays for some sweet, elderly recluse made her feel warm inside. Baking, singing, decorating a fragrant tree, sharing . . . she closed her eyes to visualize the scene.

Painful childhood memories sabotaged her exhilaration. She saw a much younger Holly, with waves of salon-styled red hair cascading over a shimmering green satin dress. She'd been overwhelmed by expensive toys and do-not-touch ornaments and terrified of the hired Santa that coaxed her into his arms. She was seven, but the moment had remained frozen forever in her heart. Sitting on a stranger's red velvet lap, she had looked over at her parents and their guests, and for the first time in her life, felt totally unloved and totally alone.

"Volunteer Bureau, may I help you?"

She was jarred by the cheerful female voice. "Yes. My name is Holly Peterson, and I want to sign up for the Chain of Caring project," she stammered. "I saw the spot on TV."

"Wonderful. Let me explain how the project works, and then I'll need to ask you some questions." The coordinator emphasized the need for a four-month commitment to an "adoptee" and described the types of errands and chores most frequently requested.

"All right, Holly. Can you tell me something about yourself that might help me match you up with one of our clients? We like to know about special talents, skills and personal interests."

"I'm a cosmetologist. I do make-overs. I usually focus on makeup consultation, but I can cut and style hair and do facials, manicures, pedicures, what have you." Holly could hear the sound of computer keys clicking as she spoke, and she assumed her talents were being categorized. "I like to cook. I took care of my mother while she was ill, so I have a little experience with bedside care and special diets."

"Do you enjoy celebrating Christmas?"

Holly paused to examine her motivations. Was she searching for the holiday of her dreams? A fantasy Christmas where sharing time and seeing loved ones was more important than the giving of gifts? The pause became an uncomfortable silence. She moved the phone to her left hand.

"I've always—" she hesitated to find the right word "—spent Christmas with my mother, and she died last January. I'd love to have an old-fashioned celebration with my adoptee."

"Wonderful. Do you consider yourself a patient person, a good listener?"

Holly brightened. "I have to be," she replied with a laugh. "I listen to people's problems all day. Not that I'm complaining—I rather enjoy it. I consider myself a people person."

Holly answered several questions about time and availability, and then asked a few questions of her own. The computer hummed for a moment.

"Perfect. I think I've got someone." The young woman sounded pleased. "It's only fair to be honest. We've had a hard time matching this one up. Your client is an elderly diabetic on oral medication who lives in a remote area in the West Hills. He needs companionship, and he can't stray too far off his diet, not even for the holidays."

"And his name?" Holly asked.

"Snow. Mr. Emmett Snow."

"I have a confession to make."

Intrigued, Nick Petrovich came to rest in a sitting position on his rowing machine. He'd been working out, waiting for the morning business report, when the public service announcement caught his attention. His breathing slowed as he watched the thirty-second spot.

"Call to register with the Volunteer Bureau."

It was a nice thought, helping someone through the winter months. He memorized the number, then returned to his vigorous rhythm on the machine.

"Damn!" Nick muttered beneath his breath. He knew what was eating at him, though he'd been trying to ignore it. His grip on the curved handles tightened as he thought of his parents. They had called from the family home in Chicago to announce that they had planned, without consulting him, to visit the old country during the holidays. In their thick Croatian accents, Anna and Stephen Petrovich told their only child he would have to spend Christmas without them, but the three of them would be together in spirit.

In spirit? Nick snorted at the thought. He'd returned home to Chicago every year *in the flesh* since he was eighteen to celebrate Christmas. Once a year he embraced the old-world traditions and mingled with loud, demonstrative relatives. But there would be no gathering this year.

He admitted he'd made fun of the old ways and spent a good part of each visit reminding his parents how embarrassed he had been as a kid, receiving homemade gifts while his friends picked toys from catalogs. Wasn't that human nature? Last year he'd made a sharp remark and turned in time to see the hurt expression on his mother's face. It had wrenched his heart. In trying to explain his feelings, he'd made a mess of things, wavering between Croatian and English, between dutiful son and independent man.

Picking up a towel, Nick wiped his forehead and neck. Did his folks see his affluent life-style as a rejection of their humble immigrant roots?

The guilty feelings persisted even after he showered. He perused the morning paper while he microwaved and ate a short stack of frozen pancakes. Every time he ran down a listing of stocks, the phone number for the Volunteer Bureau came to mind.

Adopting a client for four months would be personally fulfilling. He recalled the meager holiday celebrations of his youth. The hard times were long over. He sent checks home to his parents every month and had money to spare. Money that would brighten some elderly shut-in's winter months. He was blessed and wanted to share his blessings. And he didn't want to spend the holidays alone.

He dialed the number and listened to the young woman's explanation of how the Chain of Caring project worked.

"I'm new here, Mr. Petrovich, and a little slow on the computer," she apologized. "Can you tell me something about yourself and your interests?"

"I'm an architect who writes programs for use in design, and I work as a consultant to architectural firms in the implementation of my programs. I enjoy teaching people, so I guess that makes me a rather patient person."

"Are you a good listener?"

"I grew up in Chicago, in one of those neighborhoods that resembles the U.N. I learned to listen with both ears and to respect older people."

"Not so fast, please. I'm having trouble inputting everything into the computer. Okay. Do you enjoy celebrating Christmas?"

"Yeah, I love shopping and giving gifts," Nick replied quickly. "Mistletoe and holly and silver bells. Got a client lined up for me yet?"

"Let me find the right commands here. Hmm. Petrovich. P—E—T—ahh—looks like I'm coming up with a match. This is the first time I've done this, actually, it's kind of fun. Let's see, here's what the computer recommends."

"The name?"

"Snow. Mr. Emmett Snow."

One

Good to see you again, Mr. Petrovich." The young man behind the deli's checkout counter smiled before he began adding up Nick's purchases. "You don't usually come in here on Friday nights. Monday and Thursday, isn't it?"

"You're right. Monday and Thursday." Nick shook his head in disbelief. He knew the fashionable West Hills deli was proud of their family-owned business and personalized service, but did they really memorize names and shopping patterns? "I'm surprised you remembered me so clearly."

"It's easy. You always write checks, and you got a name that's hard to forget." The young clerk mentioned the total to Nick, then began bagging the takeout food. "On top of that, you've been coming in for three weeks, and you always buy what appears to be dinner for two. Don't take offense, but I figured you were dating someone in the neighborhood who likes to eat our cooking twice a week.''

"Not quite," Nick corrected with a laugh. "I'm a volunteer, helping a guy named Emmett Snow with a few things. He can't get out as much as he used to—" Nick stopped, seeing the startled look in the young man's eyes. "It's rewarding," he added with a shrug as he finished writing his check.

"Emmett Snow?" The clerk's eyes were wide. "I don't mean to be rude, but that guy's a grouchy old hermit. Back when I started as a box boy for my father, the kids called him 'Frosty.' I can't imagine him accepting help from anyone."

"Emmett's a bit stubborn," Nick conceded, slipping his checkbook into the inside pocket of his overcoat. *Stubborn?* His adoptee was a cantankerous, domineering pain in the behind, but Nick was determined to win him over before the holidays started. "I've hired someone to rake the leaves, clean the gutters, and we need to work on weatherproofing the old house."

"Well, good luck with your project. You must be some kind of smooth talker, Mr. Petrovich. You couldn't get most people to say boo to Ol' Frosty." The young man threw a couple of mint candies into the bag. "Here. Compliments of me. I like meeting people with courage."

Minutes later Nick parked his Mercedes, gathered the grocery bags in his arms and stepped out into the inky darkness. As he made his way up the long stone path leading to the front stairs and main entrance, he thought about Emmett's need for a security light to illuminate the yard and walkways.

As Nick reached the porch, the sound of metal on metal attracted his attention. The noise seemed to be coming from the side of the house.

Setting his groceries down and stepping out onto the grass, he caught sight of a tall figure wearing a stocking cap and heavy jacket emerging from the dimly lit toolshed. The intruder moved into the pool of light near the woodpile, and Nick felt his heartbeat quicken as the details grew clear. The trespasser was testing the weight of an ax in gloved hands.

As Nick thought of Emmett Snow's vulnerability, his body went on full alert. Spotting a garden hose nearby, he picked up the gun-shaped nozzle, edged toward the woodpile and tried to blot scenes from every horror movie he'd seen from his mind.

"Freeze! We've got you covered!" Nick shouted, using both hands to brandish the chrome pistol nozzle with all the flair of a TV cop.

The attacker turned for a frontal assault, raising the ax high overhead. With the stocking cap pulled down to eyebrow level and a weapon at the ready, the heinous criminal's appearance was formidable.

"Put-the-ax-down!" Nick enunciated each word slowly, then took two steps forward. He felt the weight of the hose, trailing behind him in the grass like a slithering snake. "Don't force me to use this!" he growled in warning. A fragmented Croatian prayer ran through his mind as he steeled his nerves and took another step.

The heavy ax wobbled precariously. "Watch out! I just sharpened it!" the homicidal thug screamed as the ax head fell forward into the sawdust.

Caught up in the frenzy of the moment, Nick aimed the nozzle at the apparent sociopath and pulled the trigger. A trickle of water gurgled out in a weak stream.

In the silence that followed the intruder took off the stocking cap and revealed a tangle of burnished, shoulder-length hair. It was a woman. A rather beautiful woman.

"Excuse me." There was a sarcastic edge to her voice. She rested her hand on the ax handle. "I think your gun has just sprung a leak."

At that moment Emmett Snow jerked the back door open. "What's all this yellin' and carrying on, Holly?" he demanded angrily. "I sent you out here to round up some kindling—"

"I thought she was an intruder, Emmett." Nick moved toward the woman.

The older man's gaze flashed to the shiny nozzle, then lingered on Nick. "Petrovich! Nick! What the hell are you doing here? You trying to put out a fire or helping Holly start one?"

Holly looked at the array of forbidden foods Nick Petrovich had set out on the kitchen table.

"There's enough for the three of us," the tall, dark-haired man assured her. "Are you still upset? I must have apologized three times—"

"Four," she corrected, suppressing a smile. He was obviously embarrassed about the scene he'd created outside. He'd slipped out of his camel-hair coat, rolled up his shirtsleeves and spent fifteen minutes splintering wedges of wood into kindling as a peace offering.

Mistaking her for an ax murderer was forgivable, but the potpourri of take-out food was something entirely different. Then there was the issue of two volunteers sharing one adoptee, and finally, the problem of this man's overwhelming presence. It wasn't enough that he emanated self-confidence, success, intelligence and good humor, but he kept meeting her gaze with those incredible brown eyes.

Nick Petrovich. There was an ethnic quality about him, but was it his face, the tone of his voice or his gentle persuasive manner? She had to ignore all that for the moment and address the problem of Emmett Snow's diet.

"Nick, it's really nice of you to buy these take-out delicacies for Mr. Snow, but sweet-and-sour sausages and apple strudel and, well, ninety percent of this meal isn't on his diet."

"What diet?" Nick opened another white carton.

"Mr. Snow is a diabetic on oral medication. Didn't he tell you?"

"Well, I got the fire going," Emmett interrupted from the doorway, rubbing his palms together. "Glad you brought the food. Holly was going to feed me shrimp salad and a bran muffin."

"What's this about a diet, Emmett?" Nick looked at the elderly gentleman, silently adding the word crafty to cantankerous.

"Nonsense, two or three nights a week of real food won't hurt me. I've been enjoying your visits, and it doesn't ruffle my blood sugar too much. Holly, why don't you join us for supper?"

"*I* visit you on Friday nights." Holly gave the shrimp salad an extra toss. "Shouldn't you be inviting Nick Petrovich to join *us*?"

Nick and Mr. Snow exchanged a conspiratorial glance. "Why don't we all just invite ourselves to sit down, have a little smorgasbord and get acquainted?" Nick suggested, handing Holly a paper plate.

"But what about Mr. Snow's diet?"

"Let me indulge him a little," Nick said with a wink.

They ate their meal in the living room in front of the blazing fire. Holly used the opportunity to study her fellow volunteer. He smiled easily and often, so her attention was drawn again and again to the lower portion of his face—the determined set of his jaw and the generous mouth, which was so often curved in a beautiful smile. Each time Nick combed his carefully styled hair back with his fingertips, dark brown wisps fell onto his forehead, softening the classically handsome lines of his face. The flickering firelight only heightened the aura of warmth that surrounded the man.

"So you do make-overs in the salon, but you also free-lance for television and do location shoots for movies?" His eyes reflected interest. When she gave only a brief response, he nodded as if to encourage her to say more.

"Holly fusses a lot," Emmett interrupted. "She insisted on cutting my hair today and did a fair job of it. Gave me a pretty good shave too, then she made me mad when she worked on my fingernails and toenails. A man's nails are his private business."

Holly didn't answer. She knew her adoptee appreciated the attention. He'd even admitted that diabetics were supposed to take good care of their feet. Being with Nick seemed to bring out some inner need in Mr. Snow to be macho. She tried to understand the phenomenon and hide her resentment.

Nick studied Holly's expression as Emmett talked about the volunteer work she'd done. Shopping, preparing meals and freezing them, one-on-one care. She looked ethereal at the moment, the rich auburn waves of hair backlit by the fire, creating a halo of red-gold around her heart-shaped face. It was as if her outer appearance reflected her inner beauty, a sense of caring evidenced by everything she'd done for Emmett. Nick felt a tinge of envy as the older man's tone softened and he said something about blood-sugar monitoring. Why hadn't Emmett asked him to do that?

"Now, Holly, you should hear about everything Nick's done around here. He hired a company to rake the leaves and clean the gutters and another one to do the chimney." Emmett bit into the tiny sliver of apple strudel on his plate. "And he insists on paying for getting the old house weatherproofed so I won't freeze to death in these drafty old rooms."

"You're very generous." Holly addressed the compliment to Nick. "But I think we might have a problem. We have two volunteers and one adoptee—"

"I was thinking about that. Must be our last names. Petrovich and Peterson. They had a new person on the computer the morning I called, and I bet their data bank uses the first three letters of the last name and well, computer error. We've both been coming here three weeks without knowing the truth, and Emmett never said anything. There aren't any other volunteers hidden away, are there?"

"Hell, no, and I didn't say anything because I need the both of you!" Emmett Snow wadded up his napkin. "One volunteer ain't enough."

"But Mr. Snow, what about—" Holly set her plate down and leaned forward. "What about Thanksgiving and Christmas? You'll have to choose between us—"

"No problem," Nick interrupted. "I'm willing to spend both holidays with Emmett."

"So am I," Holly countered. "In fact, I was looking forward to it."

"Maybe the three of us can spend the holidays together, and until then, you and I can work out some alternating schedule so we don't spoil our adoptee."

"Spoil? I'm not some piece of fruit, you know!" Emmett threw his napkin onto the rug.

"You're right." Nick stood and picked up the napkin. "There's no such thing as too much attention."

"But there are different forms of attention." Holly picked up the plates and headed toward the kitchen. "And you might want to look up the meaning of the word *indulgence*, Mr. Petrovich. Would you like to help me put some coffee on?"

Nick gathered utensils and napkins before joining her in the kitchen. "Look, we're both links in the Chain of Caring." He accepted the can of coffee she handed him and began measuring spoonfuls into the filter. "This isn't a competition. It's obvious we each have unique talents to offer Emmett."

"Why is it that he allows you to call him Emmett and he's asked me to call him Mr. Snow?"

"I don't know. Propriety, perhaps. Or male bonding. I wouldn't complain, he allowed you to cut his toenails."

"I'll let you do the honors next time, if you're not too busy with your male bonding." Holly laughed at Nick's use of the buzzword, and he laughed with her. The sound made her like him even more.

Holly watched as Nick dumped eight spoonfuls of coffee into the filter, then she cleared her throat.

"Like your coffee rather strong, do you?"

"I usually use instant to tell you the truth."

"It shows. You can cut back a bit. I think even five heaping spoonfuls might put hair on our collective chests."

He stared at her for a long time. "Do you like men with a lot of hair on their chests?"

"Not really." Holly noted the smooth expanse of skin where Nick's shirt was open, the light feathering of hair on his exposed forearms. "It's just an expression."

"All right, back to the subject of competition. I have my way of doing things, and you have yours. They're fairly compatible. I think we could combine our efforts."

"Even so, Nick, we can't let Mr. Snow get too dependent on us. We have a four-month commitment to him, and then he'll be alone again." Holly poured water into the automatic coffee maker while Nick slipped the filter bin into the slot. "I think this is a great opportunity to make him realize he can still take charge of his own life."

"I agree." Nick reached over and turned on the switch to the coffee maker. He leaned against the counter and folded his arms across his chest. Holly discarded the paper plates in the garbage and began tossing out the little white deli boxes. She was wearing faded denims that molded to her curves and emphasized her long legs. Her pink windowpane sweater was sporty but elegant. Perfect for giving a seventy-two-year-old man manicures and pedicures . . .

But Nick didn't want to talk about Emmett Snow, he wanted to ask about Holly Peterson. Why had she volunteered to help an elderly shut-in? Didn't she have a family or a social life? And what about the hectic schedule she'd been describing?

Holly turned around. "I suppose we'll need some cups for the coffee. They're in the cupboard right behind your head."

Nick made no effort to move. He stood planted in front of the counter, watching her and smiling. "I was thinking, Holly." His voice was low and soft. "We might *want* our schedules to coincide now and then. I've enjoyed your company tonight. It's the first time I've ever been happy about a computer error."

Holly stood opposite him, her back hugging the counter. She'd dialed the Volunteer Bureau because she didn't want to be alone for Christmas. After meeting the irascible Emmett Snow, she was resolved to break through her adoptee's harsh exterior before the holidays. Meeting her fellow volunteer had complicated things. She didn't know whether to view Nick Petrovich as a rival or another sort of resolution. A man who could help her celebrate Christmas with all of her heart.

"I wouldn't mind having our schedules mingle now and then, either," she said quietly.

Two

_____

The usual?'' Sara Tanaka twisted a tendril of Holly's long hair around her finger. "Dry cut. Trim the ends, a little off the top, tidy the waves close to the face?''

"Do you have to make me sound so damned predictable?'' Holly feigned anger at her coworker. Sara was the only person to whom she entrusted her hair—and her innermost feelings.

"Sorry. Maybe it has something to do with the fact that you've seldom deviated from those very specific instructions.''

"I'm not upset with you, Sara. It's _me_.'' Holly looked at her reflection in the mirror. To the horror of her parents, she'd inherited the vibrant red hair that had skipped two generations of her mother's clan, the McMillans. And to make matters worse, the red was combined with the Peterson family's genetic curse—voluminous waves.

She'd been determined since adolescence to cast aside her parents' negative comments, to replace them with her own positive outlook. But there were moments when those early insults resurfaced and she invested all of her energy telling herself she'd been blessed with a rare gift—a natural sponge, red.

She'd outgrown much of the frizz and the bright red had darkened to a rich auburn, but the insecurities still haunted her from time to time.

"I feel like doing something different," Holly mused, touching one of the long kinky waves that fell to her shoulders. "More height, maybe."

"You have plenty of uh...height, Holly." Sara began lifting up sections of hair and studying them thoughtfully. "Something bothering you?"

"It's hard to work in a salon specializing in makeovers without giving some thought to making a drastic change."

"Adding height isn't what I consider *drastic*. And don't give me that weak excuse. You've worked here for years without going through a total overhaul. Something prompted you. You've met someone, haven't you?"

"Mind reader!" Knowing the hour was late and she was alone with her longtime friend and confidante, Holly decided to divulge the truth. "He's a fellow volunteer. We're both helping the same shut-in. It all started when I had an ax to grind." She smiled to herself. "Literally."

Holly related the story of the first meeting with Nick Petrovich near the woodpile and the meal they'd shared with Emmett Snow in front of the fireplace. "Nick's hours are flexible like mine, so we'll be spending some time together, especially at Thanksgiving and Christmas.''

"And?" Sara prompted between snips of her scissors.

"And he's got something I like very much in a man."

There was a long pause.

"Holly! What is it?"

"Okay, okay." Holly laughed at her friend's exasperation. "Nick has heart. At least that's the impression he's given me. He's an architect who creates computer programs, but he's not one of those analytical, left-brained *wunderkind*. He seems to use both sides of his brain, very well—"

"First you talk about his heart, then his brain," Sara interrupted, her scissors held in midair. "I'm interested in hearing a few details about the exterior of this man. Like body type, hair color, eyes."

"Tall but not too tall. Well muscled without bulk, nice broad shoulders, dark brown hair and eyes. Thoughtful eyes with long lashes and expressive brows."

"Clean shaven or fuzzy faced?"

"Spoken like a professional cosmetologist. Clean shaven."

"Nose and mouth?"

"Hmm. The nose may have been broken—"

"Broken while defending some underdog, no doubt. You said the guy has heart. Go on. You haven't described his mouth."

"He has this mysterious little smile..." Holly wanted to close her eyes and remember every detail of her first encounter with Nick. "But I'm being foolish," she said with a sigh, addressing not only Sara's reflection in the mirror but her own. "I'm making him sound flawless, and there are flaws."

"Uh-oh, here it comes. There's a frog growing on top of his head." Sara chuckled as she pulled a clip from Holly's hair and stood back to check her progress.

Holly studied her friend while holding still for the inspection. She'd always envied Sara. Her coworker shared warm relationships with a multitude of siblings and had married into an even larger family. Her frequent mention of these close ties only served to remind Holly of her own lack of family.

"You mentioned a flaw, Holly."

"It's not really a flaw, but it could be a problem. Nick's too generous. You know how I've always said I'd like to share my life with a man whose ambition doesn't smother his ability to enjoy the simple things in life?"

"I remember you saying something like that once, but I didn't think you actually meant it."

"I did mean it. And that's where the problem comes in. Nick is too indulgent."

Sara responded with a frown. "But on the other hand, I thought you liked a man with heart."

"I do, but there are gifts from the heart and then . . . there are gifts."

"Who are these people?" Holly shouted over the clamor of drills and hammers.

"Nick hired 'em." Emmett Snow hollered back from his easy chair. He rattled his newspaper for effect. "Call themselves insulators or some fool thing. I call 'em infiltrators! They're supposed to help me keep the house warm this winter, but they keep leavin' the front door open to do their work!''

"Look at you. You're shivering from the cold, Mr. Snow," Holly admonished as she put down her grocery bag. She helped him into a bulky sweater and slipped an afghan over his legs, then looked around the living room, noting the progress of Nick's philanthropic mission. The workmen were installing double-paned storm windows, an adjustable threshold, weather stripping and an insulated glass screen around the fireplace.

This was Tuesday, one of *her* days, but it was evident Nick had kept his word and taken steps to see that their volunteer schedules coincided.

"What's the hammering in the basement?" she asked Emmett.

He was busy rooting through the grocery bag she'd set down beside his chair. "They're putting that fiberglass insulation under the floors. Amazing, isn't it? When Nick Petrovich thinks of somethin', he simply hires the folks to do it. I just wish they'd go about their business quietly, like you, Holly."

"Thank you, and stay out of the groceries," she scolded. "Now where is the amazing Mr. Petrovich?"

Her wily adoptee pulled a wheat cracker from a box, bit into it, then flashed a defiant smile. "Nick's in the kitchen talking to some fella about remodeling."

"Remodeling? He's disrupting the whole house!" Holly bent to pick up the groceries. "I was hoping we'd get a chance to talk about the meal plan for this Thursday."

"This Thursday?" Emmett cocked a hand around his ear. "I can hardly hear you with all this hammerin' and yammerin'."

"Thanksgiving!" Holly shouted before heading toward the kitchen.

Nick was bent over, studying sheets of graph paper spread out on the counter. "So, on the third plan you're suggesting we knock out the wall to the pantry to make room for the island?"

A balding older man tapped his finger on the design. "That's one possibility. See, it would give you an extra foot for the wraparound counter if you want to go that way. But it sounds like you're set on keeping that old oak table."

Holly settled the groceries on the opposite counter and waited for a pause in the conversation.

Nick was dressed in a designer sweater, a subtle geometric design of burgundy, gray and navy blue. His gray cords made the outfit appear more casual, in sharp contrast to the business suit he had worn the first time they'd met.

After years of working with make-over clients, Holly was trained to be observant when it came to clothing trends and designer labels. She had a feeling that her sophisticated covolunteer was equally aware and equally observant.

"Hello, Nick," Holly ventured when there was a lull. "What's going on?"

He turned. "Holly." The word was more of a statement than a greeting and was accompanied by a sheepish grin. "I was just getting some estimates for a little remodeling. This is Bob Reedsport. He's a contractor."

"Nice to meet you," Holly said curtly as she nodded at the stranger. "I didn't know Mr. Snow was unhappy with his kitchen."

"He isn't," Nick said with a shrug as he picked up one of the designs and studied it. "But I think you'd have to admit the colors are drab and the layout isn't convenient. The linoleum's torn in places. Emmett could trip, fall and break a hip."

Holly looked down at the floor. Nick was right. A worst case scenario flashed through her mind. Why hadn't she noticed the danger herself?

"I was looking at his old electric stove," Nick continued. "The thing is an antique and potentially dangerous, especially when you consider Emmett's failing eyesight. I thought a new model—" Nick stopped in midphrase. "I'm doing it again, aren't I, Holly? Overdoing it would be more exact."

"No, no, the weatherization was a great idea." Holly pulled the woolen scarf from around her neck. "The house was definitely drafty. It's just that a kitchen, well, a kitchen's more personal. Don't you think you should involve Mr. Snow in the planning stages? Maybe he doesn't want anything changed. And then there's the disruption and the expense."

"I'm working up an estimate for the third plan now," Bob Reedsport muttered as he punched numbers into a calculator on the counter. After settling a pencil behind his ear, he named a figure. "I know it sounds high, but that includes materials, rewiring, new pipes and labor if you go with Plan C. The paint job is still up in the air depending on specifics. Now about the old wallpaper..."

Holly was staggered by the amount of money Nick was willing to invest in their client's cause. She felt outdone. More than outdone, she felt conspicuously inadequate. What had she contributed today other than a bag of groceries and an offer to cook liver and onions, Emmett Snow's favorite meal?

Nick and Bob Reedsport continued their discussion while she put the food away. She loved this kitchen. It wasn't drab, it was muted. Of course, she agreed unsafe items like the stove and linoleum should be replaced or repaired, but what about the homey, lived-in atmosphere? The kitchen was the heart of any home. How could Nick consider doing open-heart surgery during the holidays?

When she turned, Nick was shaking hands with Bob Reedsport.

"I'll get back to you soon, Bob. Thanks for suggesting the fourth option."

After the contractor left, Holly poured herself a cup of coffee. "Out of curiosity, what are these options?" she asked.

"First there's Plan A." With a wave of his hand, Nick beckoned to her, then stepped aside to allow her a closer look at the design. He talked her through the details of the three basic plans.

"Then there's the fourth option," Nick added quickly as he rolled up the sheets of graph paper and secured them with rubber bands. He poured out his tepid coffee, refilled his cup and sat down at the round oak table in the corner of the room.

Feeling compelled to join him, Holly sat down, too. She prayed the final plan wasn't as complicated as the first three. "What's this fourth option?"

"First, I could have a new stove installed by a reliable dealership, and secondly, I could hire someone to do just the flooring. They'd have to pull up the old linoleum, prepare the surface and put down vinyl tiles.''

"Or you could install the floor yourself?" Holly blurted out. The project sounded like fun, something they could do together. "I could help you. I'm handy with tools, and I've seen the commercials on television where people install those floors in a few hours. You might be surprised at how easy it is.''

Nick's response was surprisingly terse. "I don't like surprises. Besides, Bob Reedsport said it could get complicated. This house was built in the twenties. I'd rather hire an expert who's used to working with older structures.''

"I didn't mean to imply you aren't capable of installing complicated flooring, Nick. I just thought—''

"You probably thought it would be easy." Nick took a sip of coffee and glanced up at her. There was a long silence as he studied her intently. Then he shook his head and spoke in a subdued tone.

"I grew up in an extended family of fix-it men who drove their health into the ground with their constant attempts to repair everything themselves. My father worked a twelve-hour shift at the foundry, then came home and tried to maintain the failing plumbing and wiring. And then there were wallpaper projects that took two months and ended up looking like they'd been done in half a day." Nick swirled the coffee in his cup. "I'm in a position to hire help now, to have things done professionally.''

When he glanced back up at her, Holly was shaken by the fierce pride in Nick's dark eyes. When he smiled, his expression softened.

"Sorry," he said in a low murmur. "I didn't mean to sound so dramatic, Holly.''

"Sometimes the truth holds a bit of drama." She thought of her own background. "I like the fourth option. It won't cause a lot of commotion for Emmett Snow, and we won't have a lot of strangers in the house."

"And you have a soft spot in your heart for old-fashioned houses, right?" Nick ran his palm across the worn oak surface of the table.

"I bought a Victorian in northwest Portland three years ago and sank a lot of time and money into the renovation. I like the character that's built in to an older home."

"You really don't care for the idea of tearing this room apart, do you?"

"Am I that transparent?" Holly captured the heat of her coffee cup between her palms. The chill brought on by the living room project had invaded the whole house. In the back of her mind, she wondered if Mr. Snow was cold. "This kitchen has a feeling of warmth and security. I could get lost in the pantry with the smells of all those spices." With a sweep of her arm, she took in the entire room. "And look at this. Other than the coffee maker, there isn't a single modern convenience in sight—"

Holly stopped as her eyes rested on the new microwave oven sitting atop an elaborate wooden cart in the far corner. How could she have missed it? Of course, her attention had been focused on graph-paper sketches, thoughts of remodeling and paint samples. "You bought him a microwave?" she demanded.

"Hmm. I thought it would be handy for Thanksgiving and the holidays."

"Of course." She was too shocked to speak coherently. *Money.* Was that Nick's solution to everything?

"And with the stove being so dangerous," he added, "using the microwave might prevent an accident."

Holly stood up and walked over to the shiny new appliance. "It looks complicated. Lots of buttons and special features."

"Top of the line."

His voice came from beside her ear. Holly turned to find Nick studying her. Again. For a man who knew how to turn a silent house into a noise factory, he moved with an eerie stealth.

She stepped over to the coffee maker to refill her cup. "I think we should discuss the menu for Thursday."

"Make a list of what I need to bring, and I'll be here, Holly, with bells on. But I'd better go check on the insulation crew now." He turned at the doorway and smiled. "I can run to the deli and pick up something for Emmett's dinner. Nothing that isn't on his diet, of course."

"It's nice of you to offer, Nick, but I promised to make liver and onions for him tonight. You're welcome to stay, but I'm afraid I didn't buy enough for the insulation crew."

"They all leave in an hour, and I doubt if we'd get a consensus on liver and onions as a favorite dish, anyway. Do you use cardamom as a coating?"

"No, I've never heard of it. Are you a gourmet?"

"Guilty as charged."

"But you drink instant coffee? I didn't think gourmets lowered themselves to instant."

"Well, it doesn't come out of a jar," he explained. "It's a cold-drip concentrate, my own special blend. I have it made by one of the local shops, and I pick it up twice a week."

"I see." Holly nodded. Why was she so fascinated with this man? He was an eccentric snob. Or was he? Maybe she was judging him too harshly, too quickly. People with money had a right to spend it any way they chose, and so far he wasn't a slouch when it came to charitable acts. "Would you like to join us for dinner? Or would liver and onions *without* your gourmet cardamom coating be a problem?"

"Thanks for the offer, Holly." Nick held up a finger as he backed out the kitchen doorway. "I'm not a snob, but I'm taking the crew out for a seafood dinner at The Neptune tonight. I'm looking forward to it, and I have a few questions to ask them."

"Why would having dinner with a group of guys who insulate homes bother you so much?" Mitch Donnely asked as he slipped into the large hot tub.

Nick closed his eyes and remained silent for a few minutes, allowing his body to absorb the comfort of the warm jets of water. After leaving The Neptune restaurant, he'd given himself a strenuous workout in the athletic club in the basement of his high-rise condo.

Mitch, an old friend who lived in the same building, was the last person Nick wanted to talk to at the moment. A physician specializing in sports medicine, Mitch was full of free advice—on everything but sports and medicine.

"Out with it, Nick. You look upset."

"How can I look upset with my eyes closed and this contented expression on my face?"

"Well, you said something was bothering you. Talk to me, Petrovich."

"It's nothing. I had dinner with a great group of people." Nick opened his eyes. "I sensed this wonderful camaraderie. They work together as a team, and they're proud of their skills. Very professional. And they do things together outside of work and help each other with remodeling and home projects."

"You helped me assemble my home entertainment center, Nick."

"These guys built a garage together."

"Are you comparing quality to quantity here?" Mitch asked as he began doing a series of stretches. Like Nick, he was in his early thirties and an exercise enthusiast. He also had a habit of taping old injuries. Nick had found that part of the adventure of sharing a workout with Dr. Donnely was guessing which areas would be taped each week.

"I suppose I'm trying to say there was a sense of family with these guys." Nick watched as Mitch rotated his wrists in the warm water. "It made me think about my job. I'm so isolated all day, sitting in front of computers in my condo."

"You work as a consultant, teach people how to use your specialized programs," Mitch countered. "A lot of people would envy you and the way you get to deal with hotshot architects on the cutting edge. And you have something in common with these people. A love of modern design."

"Yeah, that's true. But that's only a few days out of every month, and then I leave. I go back to my home office and work alone, and I seldom see those people again except for a drink or a game of racquetball.''

"But you're a loner, Nick. I thought you enjoyed the solitude."

"I do I guess. I don't know, maybe not. A couple of these guys at dinner reminded me of my father. They were proud of their immigrant roots and so willing to help me with my questions, so good-natured.''

"What questions? What did you need help with? Our condos are completely insulated."

"I told you I was doing volunteer work. I want to replace a linoleum floor with tiles in an elderly man's house in the West Hills, and I needed to know about the kind of flooring to buy, the tools, the glue, how to judge quality and most important, how to do it without looking like a weekend hobbyist.''

"So who's going to notice?"

"A woman, her name's Holly. She's volunteering to help out the same guy."

"I don't follow. Why do you care what she thinks about the way you install floor tiles?"

"Because I care."

"About this Holly?"

"Uh-huh. She's special, Mitch. She's funny and frank, and she's beautiful. Don't ask me about her hair. I might get poetic on you right here in the hot tub."

"So what color is her hair?"

"Mitch."

"Blond? Brunette? Black?"

Nick had to smile. During the past five years Mitch had been through two marriages and four "serious" relationships. He considered himself an expert on romance.

"Her hair is red. Deep red, I guess. Long, wavy and it looks wonderful on her," Nick said. "She's tall and slender, and she sort of glows. From inside. Maybe it's the volunteer work. I know it's upsetting sometimes to realize there are other people like Emmett Snow, but it does give you a good feeling to think you're reaching out to another person."

"All right." Mitch held up his hands. "I get the message. Don't weep into the hot tub, Petrovich. So what do you plan to do? Install the flooring under the cloak of darkness or let her see how inept you can be?"

"Great friend you are." Nick grumbled. "I intend to use the advice I got from the crew tonight and visit a showroom where they sell flooring."

"And then what?"

"I hire an expert to tear up the old floor and install the underlayment—"

"Ooooh. Underlayment. You're talking like an expert already. What the hell is underlayment? It sounds like lingerie."

"It's plywood or particleboard, and you put it down to make the floor smooth."

"And then the expert puts the tiles down?"

"No, I do that myself and—" Nick took a deep breath "—I ask Holly to help me."

Three

———

Two turkeys?'' Emmett Stone's figure blocked the front doorway of his home. "I don't believe it. You each brought your own fool turkey for dinner?"

"Well, I see you're warming to the holiday spirit. Happy Thanksgiving, Emmett." Nick couldn't hold back a laugh. He and Holly had met on the porch minutes earlier, each with a roasting pan, complete with bird and bags of stuffing.

"Happy Thanksgiving." Holly echoed the sentiment without glancing at Nick. She was clearly annoyed.

"Ditto!" Emmett nodded at the two volunteers, sticking his chin out defiantly. "Hell, we can't eat two whole turkeys. It just proves you should leave the cookin' up to a woman and let the men handle the carvin'."

"Emmett, I'm not going to argue that subject right now." Nick cleared his throat forcefully. "Holly gave me a copy of the menu and a shopping list on Tuesday."

"Then you *knew* you were slotted to bring the cranberries and yams and that turkey wasn't on your list?" She pronounced the word turkey with disdain.

"It's my mistake," Nick interjected. "When I walked into a downtown deli yesterday and saw this bird, it looked perfect. I pictured the three of us gathered around the table—"

"And you forgot about the menu?" Holly asked.

"I admit I was impulsive. Maybe we can choose between the two turkeys." Nick shrugged, unwilling to dampen the holiday spirit with bickering. No doubt Emmett would do enough bickering for the three of them today. "We'd better decide fast. We've got to get one of these gobblers in the oven."

"Well, maybe the first one to arrive should have the honors." Emmett scratched his chin and continued to block the doorway.

Holly stepped forward. "I put my foot on this porch a full minute before Nick."

"Only because you took up two parking places out front with your minivan and I had to park my car up on the hill."

"I'm being silly. Being first on the doorstep isn't the important thing," Emmett remarked with a frown. "Come on in. You didn't insulate the house just so I could leave the door open for ten minutes! I'll go pluck a coupla bristles out of the broom and you can draw straws the old-fashioned way." He ambled off to the basement, leaving Nick and Holly alone in the entryway.

"And I didn't buy and defrost and lug this turkey over here just to draw straws!" Holly set the roasting pan on the floor and took off her coat.

Nick forgot about straws and turkeys and Emmett Snow. Holly was wearing a kitten-soft pink sweater that hugged her curves in an alluring manner without being overtly sexual. A double strand of pearls reflected the pastel hues of the sweater. He was mesmerized for a moment by the shimmering sight of Holly Peterson in pink.

"You look beautiful," he said in a hoarse whisper, resisting the desire to reach out and touch the soft wool. She was wearing more makeup today, and her dove-gray eyes were as luminous as the pearls. Bright with the excitement of the holiday, he thought. "You do look beautiful. And please don't think I'm just trying to flatter you into submission. It's the truth."

"Thank you." Her annoyance was diminishing. She was clearly bemused. "Submission? Do you honestly believe that one of us will surrender their bird?" Holly bent to pick up her roasting pan and began moving toward the kitchen. "We might as well humor Mr. Snow and draw straws. Whatever happens, we can go ahead and cook both turkeys. The lean meat will be great for his restricted diet, and I have an elderly neighbor who'd enjoy a portion of the leftovers."

Nick shifted the roasting pan in his arms. He felt like a turkey himself. Why had he given in to his impulses again and bought the damn bird? Worse yet, Holly might feel outdone by his gourmet stuffing and glaze, and the last thing he wanted to do at the moment was belittle her efforts. He let Holly take his bag of dressing at the kitchen door, then maneuvered his roasting pan next to hers on the oak table.

"Lord, it looks like we're lined up for a taste test. Ready for the unveiling?" she asked.

They both removed their lids with a flourish. Nick glanced at Holly's pan. Her plump bird made his contribution look paltry. He smiled. "That's a good-size Tom. How much does it weight? Thirty pounds?"

"Eighteen." She appeared engrossed in studying the contents of his roasting pan. "I didn't know squab was in season."

It was Nick's turn to sound irritated. "This is a twelve-pound bird, raised in a stress-free environment on natural foods."

"Stress free? I wonder how they kept him relaxed after they broke the news to him, you know, about his days being numbered?"

"Actually…" Nick paused and ran his finger along the rim of the pan. "The man at the deli mentioned music with subliminal messages."

"Really? In English or Turkish?" Holly looked down at the bird in question. "Gee, maybe he learned to channel turkeys from another dimension. Do you have to fill him with crystals or something?"

"Holly." A muscle twitched along Nick's jawline. "He's just an organic bird."

"Sorry, I was joking. What's all the rest of the stuff inside your pan?" She attempted to sound serious.

"It's a glaze and instructions on how to use it. Nothing special, really."

"Uh-huh. Did you realize the instructions are in French?"

Nick picked up the packet. "So they are. That could make this an interesting adventure in cooking."

The basement door swung open. "I got the straws ready," Emmett interrupted. "What kind of dressing did you two make?"

"Old-fashioned sage and celery," Holly answered quickly.

"Really?" Emmett sounded pleasant for the first time since they'd arrived. "It's my favorite." He turned to Nick. "And what did you put together?"

"Oyster...with imported truffles."

"Truffles?" Holly raised her brows and choked on a laugh. "How traditional. I'm sure the pilgrims just happened to have a tin of truffles along and the Indians suggested combining them with oysters. You're incredible, Nick. And you're smiling. What's so funny?"

"You. I like your sense of humor, Holly. I know you're upset with me, the mix-up on the menu and all, but—"

"Your oysters sound real interestin'," Emmett interrupted again, "but we gotta pick straws." He stood in front of the sink, one hand outstretched. "Whoever gets the short straw loses."

"Loses what?" Holly folded her arms across her chest.

"The chance to cook their turkey."

"Emmett." Nick used his most diplomatic tone. "Why don't we cook both turkeys?"

Holly added her support. "Nick's right. I'll use the big oven, and Nick can stick his mellowed-out Tom in the microwave. We'll cook it using the stress-free mode." She smiled up at Nick. He was frowning. "You don't want to use the microwave?"

"I don't have microwave instructions for the glaze."

"You don't have instructions in English for that glaze," she shot back. The man was impossible. Was he programmed for only one function—to impress? The organic turkey with imported glaze. Store-bought dressing with truffles and oysters! He deserved her barbed comments. "Perhaps you've hired a chef who'll arrive momentarily and interpret for you."

"Holly."

The warning in his voice caught her attention, but the spark of anger in his expressive eyes held it. Perhaps she'd gone too far.

While they stared at one another in abrupt silence, Nick shrugged out of his trench coat and draped it over the chair beside the table. Holly lowered her gaze briefly. Suspenders. He was wearing narrow black suspenders and a light blue dress shirt. With his physique and dark coloring the effect was nothing short of impressive. There was that word again. Maybe he didn't have to work at it.

Emmett Snow clapped his hands and disrupted her thoughts.

"If you two wanna stop this stare down, maybe we can start cookin'!" The elderly man shoved a very large bowl between them. "There won't be any need for arguing. I just finished mixing the dressings together. Let's start stuffin' those birds!"

"This is foolish," Holly protested as she surveyed the holiday table from the dining room entrance. "Everyone's so spread out. Why don't we all gather at one end?"

The three agreed, and the place settings were quickly rearranged, the tapered candles lit, the chandelier dimmed. Emmett Snow stood at the end of the mahogany table flanked on the right and left by his two volunteers.

"If this isn't somethin'." He shook his head and stared at the Thanksgiving feast. "Two turkeys and all the trimmings. Sure beats the TV dinner I ate last year."

"There's something else here besides food, Emmett," Nick said quietly. "Two friends."

"I didn't forget." There was a pained echo in Emmett's tone. "It's just that words don't always come easy for me. Like now. I want to thank the both of you, for your time and the food you brought and everything you've done." Emmett extended a hand to each, glancing first at Nick, then at Holly. "I-I'd like to..." When his voice broke, he cleared his throat and looked down. "I'd like to say grace if you don't mind. That don't come easy, either. I'm out of practice. Give me a minute to shake my memory."

Holly squeezed her adoptee's frail hand. He'd made a nuisance of himself in the kitchen, barked orders about the setting of the table and arrangement of the food, and he'd grumbled about the weather, taxes and his diabetes for the past six hours. That crusty, quarrelsome facade seemed to have vanished for the moment.

"If I could just remember...how does a person forget somethin' so familiar..." Emmett sighed and shook his head in frustration. Nick prompted him in a low whisper.

Holly looked across the table at Nick in profile. Earlier, he'd countered Emmett's snappish behavior with humor. On top of that he'd taken her teasing good-naturedly and tossed a few clever comments of his own in her direction.

They'd compared notes on Portland while the turkeys roasted, discovering a shared love of spicy foods, ocean beaches, hiking, cross-country skiing and the bold designs of the city's new buildings.

If someone were to ask her for biographical information about Nick Petrovich, she'd be hard-pressed to produce the basics. She still knew little about his personal life as far as concrete facts went. It was all a series of impressions and frozen moments mixed with the memory of his deep rich laughter and that mysterious smile she'd come to anticipate.

Nick laughed at something Emmett said, then turned. His eyes met Holly's gaze. Bathed in the diffused glow of candlelight, wearing suspenders and rolled-up shirtsleeves, he exuded old-world charm.

"Wait a second, Emmett. I made a mistake. I said *two* friends." Nick's tone was apologetic. "I should have said three." He reached across the table, offering his hand to Holly. She accepted it, entwining her fingers through his, completing the triangle joined in giving thanks.

"Bless us, O Lord," Emmett mumbled the opening of his prayer. By the time he ended with "amen" his voice had gathered strength, and in Holly's eyes, the elderly gentleman had grown in stature. Perhaps it was the excitement of the feast, or the magic of candlelight, or the warmth of company, but Emmett was transformed.

"Well, we can't eat if we're holding our fool hands together!" he said with a hearty laugh, loosening his grip. "Should we sit down and act like proper pilgrims?"

Holly felt Nick squeeze her hand firmly before releasing it. The mischievous gleam in his eyes and disarming smile made her pause. There was nothing proper or puritan about her fleeting thoughts.

"Why aren't you sharing this day with family?" Nick asked as he offered Holly a refill of coffee from the pot on the hearth.

He was seated opposite her on the rug in front of the fireplace. The rhythmic wheezing from the sofa across the room announced that Emmett was napping soundly.

"I don't have any family left." She held her cup out. "My mother passed away in January after a long illness. My father died four years ago when I was twenty-eight."

Nick stopped pouring. "I'm sorry. This must be a hard time for you. Any brothers or sisters?"

"No, I'm a one and only." Holly reached over and touched Nick's hand gently until the stream of coffee began again, filling the cup almost to the brim.

Nick had purchased a dietetic fruit compote for their adoptee that Emmett had decided to save for the following day. Nick had selected small pumpkin tarts for Holly and himself.

"Delicious," Holly said after her first bite. "How about your background? I bet you're from a big family."

"No. I was an only child, too, but I had so many cousins in my Chicago neighborhood, I never had a chance to feel lonely, until I hit my teens."

"What happened then?"

"A sense of responsibility. Money was tight, and I had to save for college. My folks had high expectations. I was to carry on the family name and the Croatian heritage." Nick turned to stare into the fire.

"Success is doubly important when you know you'll support your parents in their old age."

"Where are your parents now?"

"Visiting Europe and the old country for a few months."

"Sounds like you're doing a good job of giving them support, Nick."

"Financially, yes, or at least I thought so. I've sent money home every month for years and thought they were using it to make their lives more comfortable." Nick took another bite of pumpkin tart. "I told my father to call an expert when the furnace acted up, but he's been making slapdash repairs on that monster all this time. And then I assumed my mother was buying good winter coats and quality boots." He gestured with his free hand. "She's been buying secondhand stuff!"

"You didn't know this?"

"No, I found out the truth a few months ago when my folks told me they'd been putting the money into a special account all this time, saving up for a trip to Europe to visit the homeland."

"Maybe you shouldn't be so upset. They're spending your money doing what they want to do." Holly leaned against the love seat. "You made them happy, and if they needed funds, they could have dipped into the nest egg you built for them."

"Yeah, but I wanted them to have more time to relax and enjoy their retirement." Nick looked across the room at Emmett. Holly followed his gaze. A wisp of white hair showed above the afghan.

"Guilt?" she asked.

"Maybe." Nick slid his body over the rug until he was propped up against the love seat beside her. "You see, I gave my parents financial help like a dutiful son, but every time I went home for Christmas, I let them know I'd always been embarrassed about my immigrant roots. How's that for mixed messages?''

"I don't know. Sounds pretty human to me. And it also sounds like something that can be rectified when you see them again. You're lucky. When I lost my mother, there was a lot of unfinished business. We weren't close."

"Want to talk about it?"

"Not really." Holly shook her head. "It's been a special day, and I want to savor the good feelings a little while longer."

"I'm sorry. I've been talking about myself the whole time. I'd hoped to get to know you better today, Holly."

"You did. How can two people spend half a dozen hours in the kitchen, eat a Thanksgiving dinner together, wash and dry dishes and cut up leftovers from *two* turkeys without getting to know each other better?"

"You think I'm impulsive, don't you? Buying a second turkey like that."

"I think you're indulgent, Nick. Really. And I'll never forget the look on your face when Emmett mixed your dressing with mine."

"Didn't someone say at least one thing had to go wrong at a holiday feast in order for everything else to go right?" With a slow, graceful movement he cupped her cheek in his palm.

Holly looked up into his features, which were illuminated by the glowing firelight. "I've never heard it said aloud, but it sounds logical." Reaching up, she covered his hand with hers. "And so far, everything else has felt right."

Nick bent his head and kissed her with a soft, searching caress of his lips. "I'd say it feels very, very right. I've been hoping that we might be able to share more than volunteer work."

Curling her fingers through his hair, Holly brought Nick's lips back down on hers, savoring the warmth, the firm pressure of his mouth on hers, the feel of his arms closing around her.

"I don't understand why, but I've been drawn to you," he whispered, "ever since that first night. And today you couldn't do anything wrong. I love the way you look in pink, and your pearls..." He picked up the double strand and let it cascade over his palm until it rolled back onto her body. "I love the way your pearls shimmered in the candlelight during dinner.

"I don't know how you feel, though. How *do* you feel?" he asked, his breath hot against the corner of her mouth, the words dissolving into a deep moan as he kissed her hungrily.

Holly closed her eyes. She wanted to let the sensations take hold and drown out the voice of reason. But it wouldn't be fair not to level with Nick. Hadn't he asked her a question?

Holly slowly broke off the kiss and sat up. "Nick." She remained loosely imprisoned in his embrace. It was impossible to scoot out of the little corral he'd created with his legs, but she intended to speak her mind. Gently.

"I meant it, earlier, Nick, when I said you were indulgent." Her words had a breathiness to them that softened their impact. She touched his cheek and waited until she could speak clearly. "I'm sorry, but I have a problem with people who use their money the way you do. A big problem. I admire the way you support your parents, but the situation with Emmett is different.''

Nick frowned. "When I see a need, I try to fulfill it. What's wrong with that?''

"Nothing.'' Her fingers dropped down to his shoulder. The suspenders had intrigued her all night. "But you've been hiring people to weatherize and rake leaves and clean the gutters. And there was the contractor and the microwave oven, and stuffing a turkey with truffles?''

"I can afford it, Holly.''

"It's not a matter of money. I can afford the same luxuries—it's just that I choose to do it in a different way, Nick...for personal reasons.'' She edged her fingertips over to the narrow suspender strap. "I prefer to give of myself.''

"I thought I was giving of myself. It's my time, my money, my energy.''

"Of course. I'm not saying you've done anything wrong.'' She ran a finger over the elastic webbing, skittering across to his collarbone and back. "There's no wrong or right way to do volunteer work. I just think that you...'' She paused, searching for the right word.

"You think I'm overdoing it.''

"Perhaps.'' Holly let her finger glide down the suspender strap to Nick's chest. For a man who hired others to do physical labor, he was firm and well muscled. "Today at the table, when Emmett took our hands and he looked at the food, did you see the way he smiled? It was the time we gave, not the lavish display of turkey. If we had cooked a game hen, it would have been the same.''

"I doubt if we would have bagged leftovers for an hour.''

She responded with a chuckle, then curled her fingers around the elastic. "Emmett needs us, Nick. He needs the small kindnesses and the conversation and knowing we care.''

"Why can't I give him that and make repairs as well?''

It was hard to argue her point when he looked at her with those melting brown eyes, when she felt his heart beating so close to her hand and remembered the warmth of his mouth on hers. "I guess I'm talking about reaching a balance.''

"Too late.''

"What do you mean, too late?''

"I already bought new tile for the kitchen.''

"What?'' Holly pulled back on the elastic. "You're going ahead with the remodeling plans?''

"I didn't say that. And please don't let go of my suspender strap. I can't guarantee I'll be civil.''

Holly gently eased her grip.

"I bought the flooring in the color we chose from the samples left by the contractor.'' Nick fished a section of tile out of his shirt pocket and handed it to her. "You probably didn't think I remembered your preference. Anyway, the company delivered everything yesterday.''

"And then their work crew will show up and install it?''

"They'll tear up the worn linoleum and do some preliminary work so there's a smooth base called an underlayment. The tiles will be waiting in the spare bedroom."

"Waiting for what, another work crew?"

"Waiting for us. You and me, Holly. The champion tile-installment team of Portland's West Hills." Rising onto his knees, Nick reached over and put a fresh log on the fire. Flames licked the edges of the bark as it slowly ignited. "Am I getting closer to this delicate balance you mentioned?" He stoked the embers using the poker.

Holly stared at the back of Nick's head. She could almost imagine his smug smile. "What about Emmett? How will he feel about the change?"

"We're lucky. He picked the same color."

"He knows about all this? You're not only indulgent, you're sneaky."

"I take it you're still not impressed." He glanced over his shoulder at her. "Maybe a live demonstration of my skills will change your mind. Are you up for some grubby work this weekend?"

Holly stared at Nick for a moment, then shifted her attention to the flames leaping in the fireplace. She'd been upset too many times by her parents' materialistic displays. She wanted this holiday season to be special, a celebration of love and sharing. The gifts of time and self. Would Nick spoil that for her with his excesses?

"How about it, Holly?" He settled down beside her again. "The exciting smell of the glue, Emmett's roar when he sees his kitchen in disrepair for a few days?"

"I'm sorry, Nick. I have plans for Saturday with Emmett."

He looked disappointed. "Here at the house?"

"No. Actually, I made reservations for two on the old stern-wheeler back in early November, before I knew I'd be sharing him with another volunteer."

She felt a touch of remorse at not being able to invite Nick along, but it passed. They were two very different people who chose very different ways to express their concern for their adoptee. She wanted to make Saturday special, a one-on-one day of sharing without flair or extravagance.

"It's been years since Emmett's been on the Willamette, Nick," she explained. "And I thought he'd enjoy this short cruise."

"Afternoon or evening? Won't it be pretty cold on the water?"

"There's nothing to worry about. First we'll have lunch along the riverfront, then catch the boat at two. He has cold-weather clothing, and we'll be indoors looking out the windows the entire time."

"Sounds nice. He'll probably love it."

"I'm sure he will." She glanced over at Emmett's sleeping figure, then back at Nick. "He needs to get out more."

"We can install the tiles the following weekend or some other time soon," Nick suggested.

The smile was back. A shock of dark hair had fallen over his forehead. His thumb was looped casually around one suspender. The Petrovich old-world charm pulled at her.

"*If* you're still interested," he added. "You're the one who suggested working together in the first place."

"I'm not backing out. It's a date." She closed her fingers around the small sample of tile in her palm. "But *only* if you promise to wear suspenders again," she whispered.

Four

I think we know each other pretty good now, Holly. You don't need to call me Mr. Snow anymore. First names are fine,'' Emmett announced as he stood beside her on the promenade above the Willamette River.

''Yes, first names are more personal, aren't they?'' She'd been calling him Emmett for some time now, and he'd always called her Holly. But why should she draw his attention to the oversight and cast a single shadow on this perfect day?

Emmett kept one hand on his old, worn fedora and braved the brisk river wind with eyes open wide and chin thrust out. He'd been stubborn and defiant when she arrived at the house, refusing the stocking cap and gloves she offered. He relented only slightly when she insisted he button his overcoat and wear a scarf.

The second hurdle was persuading him to move out of the house and into her car. With that accomplished, the third problem remained unsolved: getting Emmett to admit and confront his fears. Why had he been so reclusive, and did he really want to change?

She'd had the opportunity to study him closely during lunch. He had aged well. She'd always considered Emmett roguishly handsome with his white hair and mustache, square jaw, brooding dark eyes, rakish smile and proud posture. In his white shirt, tie, black overcoat and fedora, he looked like an elderly statesman.

Holly suspected the air of dignity Emmett maintained at all times was a defense, an attempt to hide his vulnerability. She knew little about his past and nothing about his former profession. He never spoke of such things outright. She found herself sorting out the veiled references for clues to Emmett's reclusive existence. Perhaps the day spent together, just the two of them, would encourage him to open up.

Emmett was staring intently at the opposite shore. Portland's east side fanned out before them, ending on the horizon with blue sky and Mount Hood's snow-topped splendor.

"Been a long, long time," Emmett said gruffly. "I don't remember Portland bein' this beautiful. And everything seems bigger. Guess I've been lookin' at life through a little TV set for the past ten years. Maybe a body gets used to seeing things small after awhile." He turned around and looked westward at Portland's skyline. "The city's been growin' and changin'. And look at me. It makes me feel old."

"You don't look old, Emmett. You look like a handsome, dignified, mature gentleman." Holly squeezed Emmett's hand to reassure him.

Perhaps it was too much for one day—the trip through downtown, lunch in the waterfront restaurant, the cruise. He'd been visibly afraid of the traffic, overwhelmed by the hurried pace of the pedestrians and slow to respond to the waiter's questions at the restaurant.

She was growing concerned about Emmett's reaction to the surprise she had waiting for him on the river cruise. Swing music from his era, accompanied by dancing.

"Well, there's one thing that's much smaller," Holly chided him. "Mount St. Helens." She pointed north to the active volcano. "We lost a little bit of mountaintop in the big eruption."

"Isn't that a marvel?" Emmett squinted beneath the brim of his hat. "I used to hike and camp up near Spirit Lake. You know, I saw the pictures of the destruction on TV, but it's still hard to believe. I'll have to get a closer look one of these days."

"No problem. After the holidays I'll drive you up to the visitors' center."

"I appreciate the offer. Are there crowds up there?"

Holly was touched by Emmett's anxious tone. "No, I'm sure it's quiet this time of year." She urged him to continue walking toward the departure point. "There's one of the old stern-wheelers docked up ahead. I'm sure that's the one we're taking."

"She's a beauty. Makes me think of the old days when we'd cruise down the Columbia River to Astoria. Lord, is the sky really that blue? How's the water looking today?" He seemed to be making conversation, marking time.

"Not as calm as it could be." Holly wrestled with the hem of her long, full skirt. Wearing a short wool jacket had been a mistake. The river breezes were lifting her hemline to immodest heights. "The wind's picking up. I still have your hat and gloves in my backpack. Let me know if you get cold." She wanted to say more, but was afraid of diminishing his dignity.

A line of passengers had assembled at the far end of the promenade. Emmett stopped suddenly as they neared the group.

"I can't do it," he announced firmly.

"Emmett, what's wrong?"

"Take me home. I just want to get the hell home."

"Emmett, you can tell me the truth. Is it the river? Are you worried about taking the cruise? It's an old boat, but it's safe. They have regulations—"

"I'm not afraid of drowning in the fool river. It's the p-people." His words were hesitant as he turned away. "I'm more afraid of drowning in crowds. I thought I'd be fine, but I'm not used to being social, Holly. I've lost touch with all my old friends. I don't get out like I used to and now . . ."

"Then we'll keep to ourselves at first, all right?" She took his arm, and he walked with uncertain steps toward the group waiting to board.

"What if my blood sugar drops? What if I get shaky and confused and these folks think I'm too old to take care of myself?"

"I've got the blood sugar testing kit in my backpack. We both know how to use it. Nothing will go wrong, Emmett. Let's sit back and relax and simply enjoy the scenery." The trembling of his hand made Holly feel like a heartless tormentor.

So much for one-on-one sharing time. Panic coursed through Holly's veins. She usually considered herself a warm and outgoing person. One of the perks of her job as a make-over expert was the opportunity to talk to people, to lift their spirits and share their problems. But where was that Peterson magic now?

She put her arm around Emmett. Was it easier to calm a customer than someone you cared about? She'd failed miserably with her parents, and now they were both gone. Why didn't she have the insight to know this outing would be stressful for Emmett? The idea had seemed so perfect, and here she was, making the poor man miserable.

"I can't do it, Holly!" he whispered. "I'd better go home."

"Everyone gets nervous about new situations," she said quietly. "At home you feel secure, and you haven't been out much, so naturally you're jittery. But I'm here, Emmett. We're in control. Everything's going to be fine. In fact, there's a little surprise I didn't tell you about."

"I hate surprises."

"That's funny. So does Nick," she said with a chuckle, trying to humor Emmett. "But there's nothing to be afraid of. This cruise is for people over sixty and their escorts. I couldn't get on without you, Emmett. There's going to be music from the thirties and forties, and couples can dance if they want. I thought you'd enjoy it."

"I don't want to dance!" Emmett studied the crowd more thoughtfully. "These are old people! I might look that way, but I feel young."

"So do a lot of other people, and if you smile a little, we might be lucky enough to meet them. Come on. We'll have a great time. Trust me." She tried to pull her hand free. "Emmett, I need to get our tickets out of my pocket."

"I want to go home," he persisted. "Please."

Holly was filled with disappointment and despair. After this fiasco, she might never get Emmett to leave his house again. She wanted to tell him her intentions had been good, to apologize...

"Why don't you let me help?"

Holly turned at the sound of the familiar male voice, and there was Nick Petrovich, reaching into the pocket of her wool jacket before she could protest.

"Would you look at this?" His expression was animated. "Tickets for *three* passengers. You must have counted wrong, Holly. I guess the three of us might be able to take this little cruise together after all."

"Nick!" Emmett continued to grasp Holly's hand while he tightened the fingers of his other hand around Nick's forearm. "I'm not real sure about all this—"

"What? A ladies' man like you? There's going to be music and dancing. I have a feeling you're going to need my help to fend off the female admirers." Nick slapped Emmett on the back. "And look at this. I brought some binoculars along in case you want to get a closer look at the skyline and the mountains."

Emmett nodded but didn't react.

While Nick talked about new construction, Holly eyed his Saturday-afternoon attire—a classic leather flight jacket, white cashmere scarf and khaki chino trousers. He appeared to be dressed for adventure, as if they were about to embark on a journey down the Nile rather than the Willamette.

"You'll have to point out some of the old landmarks to us, Emmett," Nick continued. "Wait 'til you see the state-of-the-art dry dock they've put in at the port.''

Holly suddenly felt that her link in the Chain of Caring had weakened. Fine. Maybe Nick was being sincere, but he was horning in on her opportunity to share time with Emmett. Giving, sharing time. She'd settle this with him later, and he'd better not mention male bonding unless he wanted a man-overboard situation.

Nick seemed to be avoiding her gaze. As they walked down the steps to embark, he kept up his steady banter with Emmett. Their adoptee continued to grasp Holly's hand and Nick's forearm and seemed no more relaxed than he had before the younger man's arrival.

"Sorry I've got myself so upset, Holly." Emmett spoke after a long silence. "Maybe you can get my gloves for me now. Nick's wearing his. Must be pretty cold.''

"No problem,'' Holly responded, opening her backpack. While Emmett put on his leather gloves, she looked up into the dark eyes of her fellow volunteer.

"Are you sure there isn't a problem with me tagging along?'' Nick asked. "I had to pull a few strings to get the extra ticket, but I'm willing to give it up if you want me to leave. I know this day means a lot to you, Holly.'' He took the backpack from her and slung it over his shoulder. "I hesitated until I saw Emmett get upset.''

He'd seen it all from his position atop the knoll. Emmett asking to leave. Holly distraught, seemingly on the verge of tears, but persevering, comforting

Emmett with a touch of her hand, the warmth of her smile, the soothing cadence of her voice.

Holly in sunlight with her hair afire battling to keep her long skirt at a modest height. She'd lost the battle, and he'd seen more than a glimpse of her slender thighs.

"I wanted to help, Holly. I thought you could use a second party."

"You mean a third party, don't you?" She kept her tone even and shoved her hands into her pockets. "This was meant to be a party of two."

"So I'm an interloper?" He put an arm around her shoulders and spoke close to her ear. "One last time. Do you want me to leave?"

The strain she'd felt when Emmett asked to go home dissipated. She did want Nick along. There'd be times in the future when she and Emmett would be alone, but this was the first outing. If she asked Nick to leave, Emmett might be even more traumatized, feeling he'd caused a rift between his volunteers.

They were next in line.

"Tickets, please," the man in uniform asked.

"It's still up to you," Nick said softly.

Holly took the three tickets from his hand and passed them to the man. "This might sound like a contradiction, Nick, but you're an interloper and a lifesaver rolled into one rather attractive package. Thanks for coming."

Sunlight flickered through the large picture windows of the boat's main deck, casting the dancing couples in silhouette. Nick tapped his foot to the lively tune and smiled as Holly began to move her body to the beat. She was seated beside him on the wooden bench, her attention divided between the dancers and Emmett who was sitting on the other side of the dance floor.

"May I have this dance or what's left of it, Holly?" Nick stood up and offered his hand. He saw the reluctance in her features. "Don't worry about Emmett. We can watch him from the floor."

"But—"

"I can't let this music or the sunshine go to waste," Nick insisted, pulling Holly to her feet. She stopped resisting and laughed, her even white smile catching the sunlight as he swung her in a circle, then caught her around the waist with his arm.

She began moving gracefully to the beat, watching their fellow dancers, incorporating elements of their style into her movements. The long, full skirt of her dress flared, exposing an enticing stretch of leg.

Nick watched her eyes move from his face to the scene beyond him. Emmett sat with three other men near the picture windows at the front of the cabin, sharing the binoculars and, no doubt, discussing the changes in the Portland skyline.

When the music concluded, Nick eased Holly back into his arms. "The cruise was a wonderful idea. I'm glad I invited myself."

"I keep waiting for you to pull some extravagant gadget out of your pocket."

"Holly, frisk me if you like. No gadgets, presents, turkeys or truffles. You have my word."

The music began again, a melodic ballad that brought a dozen new couples to the floor. Holly moved her arm around Nick's waist, and they began to sway rhythmically.

During the previous song they'd moved faster than anyone in the room. Now, Nick mused, they were dancing slower than any other couple. His crushing embrace thrust her breasts against his chest. He moved his hand, exploring the small of her back, the narrow waist accentuated by a woven leather belt, the flare of her hips. He forced himself to stop.

They weren't dancing in some dark, private place. It was four o'clock on a sunny November afternoon. Light from the stern-wheeler's huge windows illuminated the elderly dancers around them until the swirling sea of white and silver hair grew diffused, ethereal. The room seemed aglow with light and energy.

Nick looked down. Holly was bathed in the golden tones of autumn sunshine, her hair a tangle of wind-blown red-gold waves that framed her heart-shaped face. Though her moss-green dress and leather boots were almost suitable for a safari, Holly wore them with feminine grace and self-confidence.

"It looks as though Emmett's made some friends." She smiled up at Nick. Her eyes changed from pearl gray to smoke when his shoulder blocked the light. "I was hoping his friends might include a female or two."

"He needs male companionship, too. And it's probably less frightening for him. Getting to know a woman takes time."

"Really?" Holly raised her brows. "You sound experienced in these matters. Tell me, at what point does a man feel he really *knows* a woman? When she's in his bed?"

"No, I think it happens before that. When she's in his heart."

"You're a bit old-fashioned, aren't you, Nick?"

"I've been told I tend to put women on pedestals."

"Designer pedestals?"

"Smart mouth. Whatever they are, I'm learning to lower them ever . . . so . . . slowly."

"You like dancing slow like this, too, don't you?"

"With you, uh-huh."

"You may want to ease up on your grasp. That's not speaker static you're hearing. I swear everybody's staring at us and whispering."

Nick laughed as he backed away. "We must do this again someday. In the dark when we're alone."

The whispering stopped, and Holly found herself laughing along with Nick.

They danced every song, bracing themselves whenever the wake from a barge struck the stern-wheeler.

"Holly? I'd like this dance, please."

It was Emmett Snow, looking forlorn as he handed the binoculars to Nick.

Holly smiled and took the older man's hand.

"Do you know this tune?" Emmett asked after they'd danced to the far side of the cabin. "It's called 'When I Grow Too Old to Dream.'"

"What a beautiful title."

"It was our song, Delilah's and mine. I'd forgotten that 'til now."

"Were you married to Delilah, Emmett?"

"You know I'm a bachelor." His voice was a hollow whisper. "But my Delilah was the one woman I wanted to marry. I lost her to another man when I was in my early thirties. Sad thing." He sighed and looked out the window at the waters of the Willamette. "Let me listen to the song a minute, Holly. Sometimes it feels good to feel this bad."

Holly grew quiet, allowing Emmett to retreat into his memories. When the song ended, he held her loosely in his arms. When the music began again, he didn't move. A tear glistened on his weathered cheek, captured by sunlight. Holly longed to brush it away, to ease his pain with her touch. He appeared oblivious to the dancers who swayed only inches away from them.

"Do you want to talk about it, Emmett?"

"I've told you before I'm not one for words." His voice broke. "Don't get me wrong, girl. I still feel things deeply. Makes me feel alive. Maybe that's why I like to get angry now and then."

"Is that right? Don't expect me to let you use that excuse too often!" Holly hugged him gently.

Emmett chuckled and rested his palm against her cheek. "Thanks for today, Holly." He withdrew his arm and moved toward the closest window. "I met some pretty nice fellas this afternoon." His voice brightened as he changed the subject. "Looks like we'll get together for some fishing in the spring. Bernie's got a cabin near Mount Hood, and he's promised to let us use it." Emmett rattled off a list of plans the foursome had made.

Holly glanced up and met Nick's penetrating stare from across the room. There was promise of another kind in the depths of his eyes.

Five

I wish people would walk into this salon with some vague idea of *who* they want to be!'' Veronica, one of Holly's coworkers, slammed the door of the employees' lounge behind her. Hot espresso sloshed over the brim of the cup she'd been balancing, dripping down her fingers onto the carpet. ''Damn. At these prices I just paid a quarter to burn my hand.''

''Challenging make-over?'' Holly asked quietly. She was seated in the corner of the room, perusing new product literature and waiting for her next client to arrive.

''Impossible is more like it.'' Veronica wiped her hand with a paper towel, then dabbed at the coffee on the rug. ''I'm working on a forty-year-old secretary with dry skin who's never used moisturizer or had a facial. She walked in wanting to look twenty years younger.''

"And what happened?"

"I told her the truth. That she's damaged her skin beyond repair and we'd just have to make the best of it. I gave her a decent facial. Gloria's doing her hair now. I'll sell her every skin lotion I can think of—"

"Did you look at these new product comparison charts that arrived this week? Maybe Donna can do a skin analysis first."

"I'm not going to worry about it. They're not paying me enough to perform miracles. I do makeup consultations, okay?" Veronica took a sip of espresso. Her blond hair swirled as she turned to face the mirror. "The woman will get her money's worth."

Holly felt a pang of pity for her coworker's dry-skinned customer. She'd probably be given heavy foundation, peach blush and sold a palette of eye shadows that would make her look sickly under fluorescent office light.

In the age of the quick fix Holly felt like a dinosaur. She worked with a salon of competitive, driven and sometimes ruthless people. So many of her fellow workers seemed to thrive on the compliments given by dutiful customers, and they frequently held themselves up as the epitome of good taste and style. With the exception of her close friend, Sara Tanaka, Holly felt slightly detached from the majority of the other employees.

She looked down at the coffee stain Veronica had left on the mauve carpeting of the lounge, then up at the large mirror where the tall blonde continued to primp.

One more year of planning and Holly would be able to open her own salon. She tried to concentrate on an information packet for a new collagen cream, but her thoughts returned to Veronica's terse appraisal of the secretary.

Holly had been disillusioned with aspects of her career as a cosmetologist for some time. The transformations were fleeting and superficial. Many of the people she dealt with needed a psychological lift more than a make-over, so she'd learned to be a good listener, a confidante and sounding board.

It was people, young and old, the repeat customers and fascinating first-timers, who made her work rewarding. Since her mother's death, she often found herself wishing she could do more. When she opened her own salon, she promised herself, it would be staffed with experts, skilled not only in hairstyling and cosmetics, but in matters of the heart, as well.

Holly's daydreams of self-employment, a relaxed ambience and caring employees were interrupted when Sara opened the door to the employee's lounge. "Madame X is here," she announced to Holly with a smile. "And she's brought early Christmas presents for both of us."

"Presents?" Veronica turned from the mirror. "What's with you two? You get more tips and stuff than the rest of us combined."

Holly stood up. "It might have something to do with the fact that we have repeat clients," she said with a shrug as she made a noticeable effort to step around the coffee stain.

"Madame X" was Roxanne "Roxie" Shelton; a woman in her early thirties, attractive, intelligent, successful, affluent and the city's top-rated television anchor.

The station called Holly and Sara in every six months to consult with their on-air personnel and to talk with the lighting directors. But Roxanne chose to visit the salon at her own expense every three weeks. The nature of her treatment was confidential and conducted behind locked doors in one of the private rooms in the back. Only Holly and Sara were aware of Roxanne's special problem.

"Roxie?" Holly knocked on the door. The raven-haired newswoman who answered it, hugged her and held out a gift-wrapped package.

"Small token for work well done."

"Thank you." Holly turned and locked the door. "Good to see you. I like the way you handled that series of special reports on the homeless. Keep up the good work. Are you going to be pressed for time this morning?"

"I've got about an hour."

"When is the next broadcast?"

"Tonight, usual time, but I don't know if the redness will be gone by then. It lasted eight hours last time. Under normal lighting it's not a problem, but studio lights are very telling."

"We'll give it a rest, then add some powder. No one will notice. We'd better start right away so your pores have time to breathe." Holly stirred the wax that had been heating, then applied it gently to Roxanne's upper lip. The slight moustache was becoming more evident with each visit. As the wax dried for five minutes, Holly carried on a one-sided conversation with her client.

"I know how you feel about electrolysis, but you're getting to the point where I won't be able to keep on top of the growth. And I'll have to start working on your chin."

"Grrrmmmpphhh."

"Don't try to talk. I know you don't trust any local electrologist to keep quiet about this, but if we drove up to Seattle for the day and you wore a wig—"

"Arrgg-ggarrah."

"You've got a chance to go national, Roxie. It's only a matter of time." Holly sat down beside her client and picked up Roxanne's hand. "Say you end up in Los Angeles or New York. Who's going to keep this ritual confidential? I figure it's better to have the electrolysis now before the station gears up for the February rating period. I promise you it won't hurt."

"Dddnnneeepp."

"Okay, the person who did your eyebrows years ago wasn't very gentle or tactful. Things have changed. We'll find the best in the business. I'll go to Seattle with you, Roxie. And if you're still worried about that, you can go to Los Angeles or Vancouver, B.C."

"Nnnnooomm?"

"Nome? Nome is a bit far," Holly said with a laugh. "Trust me. No one will know." She squeezed her client's hand.

Touch was important, if not therapeutic, in this business. Holly recalled the warm relationship she'd developed with her hairdresser as a child. Every other week her mother had sent her to May with instructions to "do something about that god-awful red mop." May had been her confidante and role model and had influenced her decision to become a cosmetologist.

More than anything Holly remembered the importance of being touched, reassured, loved, even if May was a stranger in her parents' eyes. The hairstylist had taught her to ignore the nicknames given by classmates and the tactless comments made by her mother. May had taught Holly to love herself.

"Gggrrunnnnpp." Roxie pointed to her watch.

"All right. Time to pull the wax off," Holly warned. "Take a deep breath and let it out. Now think of something wonderful—like that handsome co-anchor of yours." *Or Nick Petrovich dancing through sunbeams on the stern-wheeler.* The thought came from nowhere, and the image of Nick lingered, as it had several times during the days since their encounter.

"Anonymous donor?" Holly echoed. Emmett had led her to the room he called the parlor. She stood staring at what looked like video control headquarters. "You mean someone just left a color television set, VCR and assorted tapes on your doorstep this past week? No note or explanation?"

"Amazing, isn't it? And look here." Emmett pressed the remote control. "They had cable installed too! I can watch old movies and sports and news anytime I want."

"Incredible. And did this same generous soul give you the shiny new exercise bike?" Holly ran her palm over the padded handlebars and tractor seat. She had enough experience at her gym to know it was a top-of-the-line model with a forty-pound flywheel and electronic speedometer, odometer and pulse monitor.

"Amazing, isn't it?" Emmett nodded. "Must have known I needed to exercise every day to keep my blood sugar in control."

"Where *is* Nick? I saw his car out front."

"You're too smart, Holly. I told him you weren't easy to fool. He's in the kitchen." Emmett turned his attention to the remote-control unit, flipping through cable stations.

"Did he start installing tiles early, Emmett?"

"No," Nick answered from the doorway. "We're a team, remember?" He stepped forward to help Holly with her jacket.

How could she forget when he looked at her with those warm brown eyes and that smile? "I remember. It's just that teammates are usually pretty honest with each other. Emmett told me about his anonymous donor." She followed Nick out to the hall.

"Anonymous donors. Yeah, the city's thick with 'em this time of year." Nick hung her jacket on the coat tree in the entryway. "There's no way we'll be able to track the monster down."

"Funny." Holly folded her arms and leaned against the banister beside the coatrack. "You don't look like a monster."

"Emmett had to start watching something other than game shows, Holly." Nick lowered his voice and stuck his hands in his pockets. "You know, I read up on diabetes and discovered the importance of exercise. I think the electronic gadgetry will help him keep track of how much mileage he's put in every day and make it fun for him."

Nick was being perfectly sensible. Though the gift was extravagant and she resented the "anonymous donor" ruse, Holly was hard-pressed to feel angry at her covolunteer's display of indulgence. He was motivated by concern for Emmett's health . . . and he was wearing faded denims, a blue work shirt and narrow red suspenders.

Nick must have seen her eyes drop down to his chest. "By the way, I remembered your request," he said with a teasing smile as he looped a thumb around a crimson strap. "Ready to start tiling the kitchen?" He walked into the living room and, picking up a pair of paper overalls from Emmett's chair, he handed them to her. "Here. I brought these for you to cover your clothes."

Holly looked at the shapeless white garment. "The women in the television commercials don't wear them."

"I didn't buy stick-on tiles. I bought the highest quality and that means glue and glue means messy. Smile, Holly," he urged. "Maybe we can dance on the floor after we finish, as a sort of celebration."

Holly recalled their near-scandalous daylight display on the boat the week before and Nick's promise that the next time they danced, it would be in the dark and in private.

"You'd use anything as an excuse to give gifts and celebrate, wouldn't you?" Holly chided after following Nick into the kitchen. She bent down to step into the right leg of the overalls.

"But today is special." Nick looked at her with surprise. "Normally Croatians celebrate St. Nicholas Day on December 6th, but it falls on a weekday this year, so we exchange gifts on the Saturday before or after—"

"Nick." Holly paused to pull the left leg of the overalls on. "Is this the occasion behind the VCR and television and exercise bicycle? Every day seems to be special in your eyes. You haven't stopped giving gifts since I met you."

"St. Nicholas Day is different. It's the biggest gift-giving day of the holiday season. When I was a kid in

Chicago, the Croatians would play the *tambura*, dance the *kolo*, and sing.'' His expression grew wistful.

''I didn't know,'' Holly said softly. ''I should have brought you something.''

''You already have, partner.'' Nick stepped toward her and boldly zipped up the front of her paper overalls before he handed her a trowel.

''Looks like we're done.'' Nick stood back and looked at the glossy surface of the newly tiled floor. It had gone fine, he thought. He and Holly worked well as a team, though work had stopped twice due to disputes over who could wield the utility knife with the steadiest hand. They'd wiped up the tile adhesive, then mopped and waxed the floor, all by four o'clock.

''Not bad. And it's still daylight,'' Holly commented from her position behind him in the doorway.

He bent down and narrowed his eyes, inspecting the floor one last time. ''Well, was the ordeal as hellish as you thought it would be?''

''I wish I hadn't believed the images on TV. Actually, it was fun. The best part was listening to all your stories about St. Nicholas. The one about the three sisters and the bags of gold made me think you would have done the same thing in providing dowries for the poor. Your parents chose an appropriate namesake. You must be very proud of your heritage, Nick.''

''Don't canonize me yet, Holly. Frankly I don't think about my ethnic background that often. I normally go home to Chicago every December, get totally enmeshed in the traditions, then come back to Portland and return to the life I've established for myself. It's like living with a foot in two different worlds sometimes."

Holly pulled the zipper of the overalls down while he spoke. As she shimmied out of the voluminous white garment, her slender form was revealed once again. Nick recognized the sweatshirt emblazoned with a logo for the Shamrock Run, a white pattern on a field of bright green. The design changed every year, but he had the same white on green, the sweatshirt awarded runners the first year of the race, at home in his collection. They must have run together years ago, in a sea of thousands, but he still wondered how he could have missed noticing Holly.

Late-afternoon sunlight flooded through the sheer dining room curtains, backlighting her hair with an ethereal halo of red-gold.

"I don't think you can leave the old-world roots completely behind, Nick." She looked up at him, her gray eyes warm, inviting. "There's a certain attitude that lingers. An attitude I find myself liking. A lot."

"Is that right? Then perhaps we should celebrate St. Nicholas Day and keep my attitude in working order. We can't dance on the newly waxed floor, Holly—" Nick slipped his arms around her "—but maybe we can do another kind of dance. Cheek to cheek." Holding her closer, he brushed his jaw, then his lips against the high arch of her cheekbone. "Mouth to mouth." The tip of his tongue outlined the generous curve of her mouth. "And lip to lip." He tasted the inner softness of her mouth before kissing her fully, intensifying the languid heat that passed between them.

"This feels very new world to me," she whispered between kisses. Her fingertips edged down the single suspender strap above the small of his back to the waistband of his pants. With a gentle tug she pulled his shirttail out and smoothed her hands over the flesh of his lower back.

The steady hum of the exercise bike that had been coming from the front parlor ceased abruptly. Nick felt Holly tense in his arms.

"You think Emmett's all right?" she asked in a near whisper.

"He simply took a breather. That shouldn't stop us from what we're doing—"

"He might be having insulin shock. It's that time of day. I should remind him to test his blood sugar more often if he's going to be exercising regularly."

"This is one dance Emmett isn't cutting in on, Holly." Nick stroked her back with slow, lazy circles. "We've worked on tiling the floor all day. We deserve a little time to ourselves."

She gave him an enchanting smile as she eased out of his arms. "Let me just take a look. Call it intuition, but I sense that he needs something."

They found Emmett sitting on the sofa watching an old black-and-white movie.

"She's in this one," Emmett stated flatly. "I just saw her face. I wasn't sure at first, but it's Delilah."

"The woman you mentioned to Holly last weekend?" Nick asked.

"Yep. It's like seeing a ghost."

Holly sat down beside him. "Point her out to us."

"She plays the maid. This is the first course, so she'll probably be back in a minute to clear the dishes away. She was such a good actress. She shoulda' been playing the lead!"

As the fair-haired Delilah delivered seven courses and removed seven sets of dishes, Nick and Holly watched and listened to Emmett's recollection of his lost love.

"We met when we were in group theater together here in Portland. We saw each other for more than a year, and I asked her to marry me. I was tied down to the family business. Snow's Shoes. We sold boots."

Nick looked over at Holly. She had a quizzical expression on her face that most likely matched his own, but both kept silent.

"But," Emmett continued, "Delilah was honest with me. She didn't like my commitment to the business, and she had dreams of her own. She wanted to go to Hollywood to work in movies. We did a musical production, and she took a likin' to one of the dancers, older fella name of Clarence Carpenter. She explained things to me, and we agreed to be friends. A few months later they got married and moved down to Los Angeles."

"And you? You never married?" Nick settled on the arm of the sofa.

"No, I've had my lady friends over the years, but there was no one like Delilah. See how she carries that tray of dishes, as if she always knows where she's going. She had what you might call direction."

"Did you follow her career?" Nick studied the attractive woman on the screen.

"I spotted her in movies now and then. I heard she had kids eventually, and then a few years ago, maybe five years, I got a Christmas card. Her husband had died. No return address, but there was a California postmark. It was just a friendly note and best wishes."

While Holly and Emmett talked about Delilah's acting skills, Nick began to plot. If he could get more information from his adoptee and hire a private investigator in California, there was a chance he'd have a very special surprise for Emmett this Christmas.

Nick looked over at Holly. Would she consider his search for Delilah a gift of self, a gift from the heart or just another extravagance?

Six

Nick climbed the porch stairs Sunday at noon, hoping to ask Emmett Snow for more detailed information about Delilah Carpenter. During his early-morning workout Nick had visualized a happy reunion between the long-lost lovers. If he got the facts he needed today, he'd hire a private investigator Monday.

He'd also found his mind wandering to the short, intimate interlude he'd shared with Holly yesterday. In some ways she was as much an enigma as the mysterious Delilah. She gave green-light signals for their stolen moments of affection and even initiated them herself at times. Then the mood changed as suddenly as Portland's weather. When Emmett needed attention, or there was any suggestion Nick was the harder working volunteer, he found himself courting Florence Nightingale.

Nick was surprised to find Holly Peterson answering the door to Emmett Snow's house. After an awkward silence she gave Nick a halfhearted smile.

"I thought it was my day to be with Emmett." Her tone was crisp, matter-of-fact.

"And I thought we'd given up the 'your day, my day' routine." Nick closed the door behind him, shrugged out of his jacket and hung it on the coat tree in the hall. "Didn't we decide to share these times together? I mean, yesterday we installed a tile floor, watched old movies and feasted on a well-balanced meal from the deli. Why do I get the feeling you're shutting me out, Holly?"

"I'm sorry if you got that impression. It's just— well, last week Emmett asked me to help him make an Advent wreath." She was holding a hammer in one hand, grasping a handful of cedar boughs in the other. "For him, this is the first Sunday of Advent. I figured his religious beliefs were a private matter and assumed he might not want you to know."

Angered by her words, Nick thrust his hands into his pockets and looked her squarely in the eye. "I grew up celebrating feast days and holy days and attending mass with my parents. I may come across as a materialistic snob to you but—"

"Nick!" Emmett walked into the living room, holding a tangle of nylon cord in his hands. "Come on into the dining room. Holly did a great job building the wreath. Yeah, turned out real nice. Maybe you can give us a hand hanging it from the dining room ceiling."

"Hanging the wreath?" Nick was confused. "What about setting it in the center of the table?"

"Sounds fine, but you see, my father always hung our wreath from the ceiling." Emmett continued his struggle to unravel the cord. "We made the meal into a special event with the ritual of lowering the Advent wreath for the lighting of the candles, every Sunday before Christmas."

"But you don't want a fire hazard. Holly—" he turned to her "—what did *you* say?"

"I suggested Emmett leave it on the table and thought the issue was settled—until you arrived. Excuse me, I'd better check on the bread dough." She pressed a hammer into Nick's palm and placed the cut greens on top of the hammer.

"Making homemade bread?" Nick gathered the greens in his free hand and grasped the handle of the hammer firmly in the other. "Sounds like an all-day project."

"I put my heart into everything I do. And that includes human dynamics. I was pretty sure I had Emmett convinced about the wreath, but I'll let you argue the point all over again." Holly tossed the comment over her shoulder.

Two bowls of dough rested on the counter. After checking the batch of whole wheat, she punched the dough down with her fist and began shaping two separate balls for loaves.

What was wrong with her? She was ashamed of the childish behavior she'd displayed in the living room, but how could she stop herself from feeling so possessive about Emmett? Maybe there was something to this male bonding business. Why did Emmett feel the need to change every time Nick set foot in the house? The morning had gone so well without the presence of her covolunteer.

She rolled out the dough and was busy shaping the loaves when Holly sensed she was being watched—by Nick.

"My mother gets up early to make her bread and won't speak to anyone until the dough is left to rise." He was using the same tone of voice he'd used yesterday when telling stories about St. Nicholas. Did he know the powerful effect his velvet-edged voice had on her? "Mom believes anger and other unhealthy emotions enter the food."

"So you think I'm angry?" Holly tried to keep her tone even, her voice calm.

"I think you might be jealous. I'd say next to anger, that ranks right up there as a pretty unhealthy emotion."

"Fine. The bread is for Emmett. I guarantee you won't be poisoned...today." She looked up at her accuser. "What makes you think I'm jealous of you?"

"Let's be honest. We've been competing with each other since the night I met you by the woodshed." He smiled, leaned back against the counter and crossed his arms. "We've gotten to know each other better on a personal level, and I like you a lot, Holly. You know that.

"But there's a wall between us. I get the feeling," he continued, frowning slightly, "no matter what I do, you consider anything purchased at a store less meaningful than your homemade gifts."

"I never said that exactly. I was talking about the spirit of giving, Nick."

"Still, I can't help it if I have more money to spend on Emmett than you do. Wanting to indulge others seems very natural—"

Holly slammed the bread dough she'd been forming into a loaf onto the counter. Pale brown strands of dough oozed out between her fingers as she looked up to confront Nick.

"When I called the Volunteer Bureau, no one asked me about my bank account. But if you insist on knowing, I used up most of my family's savings to give my mother the best of care before she died and to pay for my father's extended illness four years ago. I realize now that's one of the drawbacks of being an only child."

"Holly—" Nick moved toward her.

"I'm not what you might consider extravagantly wealthy, but I'm far from being poor. I plan to start my own salon next year. In the meantime I make a damned good living working three or four days a week. And I've invested my money well. You know I bought a Victorian in northwest Portland and renovated it. Well, it's almost doubled in value."

She wasn't finished. How dare he question her success! "I'm proud of my career and my life, Nick. Don't demean what I've done by implying I can't afford to indulge Emmett. I choose to express myself differently."

When he moved to put his arms around her, he appeared oblivious to the sticky bread dough clinging to her fist. She opened her mouth to warn him, but it was too late.

"Good Lord, Holly." Nick clasped her arms and drew her close. "Face it. You're just as competitive as I am, and our rivalry is getting in the way of us developing a relationship. I'm not here to compete with you. I care about Emmett . . . and I care about you." He kissed the unruly waves at her temple. "Maybe the timing is wrong today. I'm sorry. It's a bit like the stern-wheeler. I think I'm interfering with the special day you want to spend with Emmett. If you want me to leave, just ask.''

The house was calmer without him, Holly thought, but the serenity had nothing to do with competition or Emmett. Nick made every room he entered seem smaller. He was watching her with intense brown eyes, waiting for an answer. His breath was hot against her cheek.

"Nick." Holly spoke in a whisper. "You have a right to visit Emmett."

"I didn't ask about Emmett." He caressed her hair gently, then burrowed his fingers through the waves. The feel of his fingertips against her scalp sent a shiver through her body. "Do *you* want me here, Holly?"

"Yes," she stammered. "I want to be with you, Nick, but there are times when I feel overwhelmed. Maybe it's all the emotions. I see Emmett and think of my mother, the good times we never had, and then suddenly I'm sharing all those secret moments of pleasure with you instead. We kiss in the kitchen, snuggle in front of the fire, hang around gathering wood. Where is this going to lead, Nick?''

"That's up to you." His hand moved in tantalizing circles over her back. "If pleasure makes you feel guilty, as if you're neglecting Emmett, then perhaps we should meet away from here."

Holly was silent as she thought of the implications. Being alone with Nick without the built-in safety of Emmett's presence? The house gave them all a sense of family. Without that protection their strong mutual attraction could ignite...

"Why don't we drive out to Clackamas County next weekend to pick out a tree for Emmett?" Holly suggested. It sounded like a safe and pleasant break from meeting at the house. "We can go to one of those U-cut farms. Make a day of it."

"Sounds like fun. We'd have to bring the tree back here that night to decorate."

"There's a great corner in the living room."

"I thought the front parlor—" Nick stopped. "Never mind. In the meantime, maybe we can try to be less competitive. Look at me, Holly. I arrived empty-handed. I'm not threatening your culinary talents or your skill in making Advent wreaths."

He pulled back. Twisted strands of bread dough connected the front of his sweater to Holly's apron. He tugged at the sticky mess.

"It attacked me," he accused in a teasing tone. "I guess Mother was right. The anger goes into the bread. Maybe you should shape this into miniature pit bulls."

Holly joined in his laughter as they tried to pluck clumps of dough from the doomed cashmere. She stepped back to assess the damage. Without warning, Nick Petrovich pulled the burgundy sweater over his head. He was bare chested. Holly felt awkward, holding a shapeless lump of bread dough between her hands as she stared at the expanse of hard, smooth, golden flesh.

"I'll have to find one of Emmett's old shirts." Nick's eyes were on her, as if he were gauging her reaction.

Her feelings were immediate, powerful, perilous. Nick Petrovich exuded raw masculine appeal without flexing a muscle. It was the lack of after-shave that struck her. He was his own man, self-confident, without the usual need to mask himself in woodsy scents.

"Yes, you'll need a shirt, but there's no hurry," she replied in a near whisper. Her comment brought a smile to his lips.

"Yes, there is." He backed out of the room. "I don't want to end up with dough on bare skin."

"No, of course not." Holly stopped kneading the bread for a second. "Emmett wanted to light the first Advent candle today."

"Really. Sounds like an invitation to stay for the big event."

"It's more than that, Nick. It's an invitation to start over."

"We already have." He stared at her a long moment, then turned and disappeared from the doorway.

Holly sat the mangled loaf on the counter and found herself smiling. Nick had made an attempt to understand her feelings, to clear the air. But instead she found the atmosphere charged with a bold new awareness of him.

"Blast it. I think I'm supposed to light one of the purple candles first. I'll be damned if I can remember a single prayer or the purpose of this ceremony!" Emmett stood at the head of the table, looking up at the hanging Advent wreath. It swung precariously over the leftover Thanksgiving turkey and salad they'd prepared for Sunday dinner.

Nick reached out to steady the circle of wood draped with evergreen boughs. Four candles, three purple and one rose-hued, were spaced around the ring. He kept a firm grip on the nylon cord attached to the pulley overhead.

Emmett addressed Holly, "I'm just glad you brought your guitar. I don't want to light a candle in a silent room."

"Mandolin." Holly corrected, then quickly strummed a chord. "I thought I'd play a Renaissance tune with a holiday feel to it."

Nick watched Holly while he gently lowered the wreath. Emmett struck a fireplace match and slowly moved the flame across the table to light one of the purple candles in the wreath.

In the semidarkness of the room it was Holly who stole the light, Nick thought. Wisps of her rich auburn hair contrasted with her fair complexion. She stared transfixed at the candle as her fingers created magic on the mandolin's strings.

Nick felt the soft sweet notes of his own desire harmonizing with the melodic beauty of Holly's song. He watched her fingers caress the strings and longed to feel her touch against his skin.

Narodi Nam Se Kralj Nebeski, "The King of Heaven is Born." The favorite Christmas song of his people came to mind, and along with the notes that haunted his memory, the realization dawned that no one would sing the traditional ballads with him this year. He thought of the *tamburitza* he kept in his bedroom closet. The pear-shaped Croatian instrument was not unlike the mandolin.

He had to believe fate, more than coincidence, had brought him to this house. He looked across the table at Emmett. The older man was smiling softly, swaying to the music, his eyes glistening in the candlelight as he watched Holly.

This was her day, her night. Nick could have taken the mandolin from her and played the songs of his parents' homeland. But why steal her glory? He found it more satisfying to harmonize than to play solo.

He looked down at the small loaves of bread on the table. There was one loaf so mangled and misshapen it looked like a baker's nightmare. Nick smiled as he studied the gnarled lump. It represented no mistake, only the catharsis that had cost him a cashmere sweater.

Seven

———

"Welcome to the Nirvana Tree Farm!" a smiling young woman shouted before she motioned Holly and Nick to the right with a mittened hand. Holly brought her compact van to a slippery stop in the muddy field serving as an impromptu parking lot.

A light snow had fallen in the hills southeast of Portland, giving the tree farms dotting the area an enchanting quality.

"Either we've stepped inside a Christmas card, or we really *have* found Nirvana." Nick sighed as he took Holly's hand in his. "Beautiful, isn't it?"

The whole morning had been beautiful for Holly, from the moment she picked up Nick in front of his high-rise condo. The scenic drive gave them the opportunity to talk without interruption.

It was the first chance she'd had to really hear Nick discuss his work, to describe how he combined his degree in architecture and love of design with his skills as a computer programmer. Sales of his software were impressive, and his programs were being used in major universities as training tools. With the assistance of Nick or one of his free-lance consultants, the design programs were being implemented in architectural firms across the country. Plans were being made for international distribution.

Nick was a man who'd shaped his own destiny by remaining on the leading edge, by taking chances, forging ahead and anticipating new frontiers of innovative design. Juxtaposed with his stylish exterior and air of success was the humility and old-world charm she'd come to love.

Nick clutched the long-handled ax they'd borrowed from Emmett's woodshed, double-checking the fastening on the leather sheath while Holly locked the van.

"Hey, folks," a gangly adolescent hailed them, tossing each a candy cane. "Welcome to Nirvana. We've got free hot coffee, hot chocolate and fresh popcorn over by the warming fire. Help yourself. There's a furnished shelter near the fire, and we've got rest rooms for customers beside the big house. And we guarantee you'll spot some deer while you're here."

Holly was overwhelmed. In true urbanite fashion she'd always gone to a city lot and bought a precut tree. She recalled the surly attendant who had waited on her the previous year. Pale yellow light from strands of low-wattage bulbs had illuminated his scowling features as he barked out prices. The young teenage boy who guided them along the gravel path today was a study in contrasts to his urban counterpart.

"What kind of tree are you folks looking for?" he asked, blowing into his palms as he walked briskly ahead of them.

"What do you have?" Nick asked.

"Douglas fir, Noble fir, Scotch pine, White fir, Norway spruce, Colorado blue spruce." The boy glanced down at their boots and smiled. "Depends on how far you want to walk and how much you want to spend."

"I feel like we're at the ice-cream parlor." Holly shrugged. "I didn't think there'd be so many choices. Can we just look around a bit and see what we like?"

"Sure." The youngster pulled a map out of his back pocket. "Here's the layout of the acreage, a list of all the trees and the price codes. You gotta pay attention to the color coding, so watch for the markers. I don't think you'll have any trouble finding a tree you like." The boy loped off toward the next arrival, pulling candy canes and a map out of his pockets.

After they'd reached the warming fire, poured hot coffee for themselves and settled on a wooden bench, Nick unfolded the map. Together, they studied the layout of the tree plantation.

"How do you feel about the Noble fir?" Nick asked. "I hear they're the most expensive, but they're the best."

"Says who?"

"My friend, Mitch Donnelly, the sports doctor who lives one floor up. He says the ornaments hang better on a Noble."

"An expert on limbs, human and nonhuman, right?"

Nick laughed and looked over her shoulder.

She studied the illustrations at the bottom of the page. Even with close-up drawings of the needles, it was hard to distinguish one type of tree from another without a degree in botany, but one illustration stood out. She pointed to the area marked D. "If you don't mind, Nick, I'd like to look at this area. I've always been partial to the Douglas fir. If we think real hard, maybe we'll figure out a way to hang the ornaments on it."

"You do have a bit of a mouth on you, don't you?" he teased, running his thumb over her lower lip. "Hmm, very nice. I can't wait to get you alone in sector D."

Holly felt mesmerized by his eyes, his touch. There was an underlying sensuality in his voice. Layer upon layer of intimacy had been building since the moment he'd greeted her with a kiss in front of his building. During the trip he'd held her hand, touched her cheek, run his fingers along the edge of her thigh.

Their coffee finished, they put their gloves back on and began walking toward sector D with occasional glimpses at the map.

"Do your folks normally put up a tree when you go home to Chicago?" Holly purposely steered the conversation away from herself.

"Every year. Of course, they've modified the old customs."

"Meaning the customs practiced by Croatians in Yugoslavia?"

"Yeah. In the old country—" Nick gestured with his hand "—people didn't have Christmas trees. My father's told me about some of the traditions he remembers from his boyhood. One important ritual involved the Yule log.

"On Christmas morning," he continued, "before the sun came up, the male members of the family went to the forest to find the perfect tree. A young oak."

"How can you find a perfect tree in the dark?"

"I never thought to ask. If I had, my father would have dragged me out to some nearby park at four in the morning to prove it could be done." Nick's expression was a plea for understanding. "You learn not to question the wisdom of the old ways, Holly."

She looked over at Nick. He was wearing a fashionable charcoal-gray wool jacket. A red scarf hung loosely around his neck. A healthy red tinged his high cheekbones, and the wind ruffled his dark hair. No matter how many times he brushed it back with his fingers, a shock of chestnut brown always fell over his brow. With the ax slung over his shoulder and his masculine gait, Nick looked as if he belonged outdoors.

She tried to picture the men of the Petrovich family walking out to the woods on Christmas morning decades, perhaps centuries ago. Were they all as handsome and self-assured as Nick?

What would it be like, she wondered, to feel your family roots so strongly?

"So after they found a young oak, what did they do?"

"They cut it down. There were traditions and rituals to adhere to, of course. For example, the tree had to fall to the east at the very moment of sunrise."

Nick's tone grew reverent, his step slowed. Holly thought it would be a poor time to voice her long-held belief that a Yule log was a type of elongated cheese ball covered with nuts.

They reached sector D and moved through the straight rows of trees, stepping back to inspect the Douglas firs for height and symmetry, double-checking the colored strips of cloth against the coded chart on the map.

"So the men of the family brought this Yule log home right after sunrise?"

"Uh-huh. The women waited in the doorway holding candles on either side to welcome the *badnjak*, Yule log, into the home. Next they sprinkled corn and wine on the log and prayed for a good harvest in the year to come."

Nick was quiet for a moment. He let the ax fall to the ground and reached through the thick limbs of the fir to stroke the bark of the tree in front of them. "What do you think of this one?"

"Nice, very nice." Holly studied the Douglas fir. "It has an attitude."

"A tree with an attitude? Been hanging around the salon too long?" Nick raised his brows as he glanced in her direction. Then his expression turned serious. "How come you never answer my questions about your home life or your family? I know your parents are gone, but you must have had some special family traditions or customs."

Holly rubbed her palms together and avoided looking at Nick. She thought of the disappointment and hurt she'd suffered so many years. Was fighting and bestowing guilt on your child traditional? Was it family custom to hire strangers dressed as Santa to entertain your daughter on Christmas Eve?

"I used to make a wish list every year." She ran her fingers over the needles of the tree they'd chosen. The branches from a neighboring tree brushed against her head, almost knocking her stocking cap off. "I made one list with catalog numbers, one without. But I never had the courage to show my parents the second list."

Nick stepped around the bushy fir, trapping her between the soft lush boughs, taking her in his arms without speaking.

"What was on the second list?" he coaxed, staring down into her eyes.

She felt enveloped in a cocoon of soft green needles, gray wool jacket and Nick's warm brown eyes.

Her answer was a wispy monosyllable. "Love. Love was the only word on the list." She could still see her childish scrawl after all these years.

"You didn't feel loved, Holly?" Nick took off his glove and touched a warm finger to her cheek. "What did they do to you?"

"It's not what they did, Nick. Maybe it's what they didn't do." Holly pulled back slightly. "Don't look at me that way, please. I don't want your pity. I don't want to dwell on the past. My parents are gone. No regrets."

"Did you ever get your wish?" His fingers touched her chin, tilting her face upward, adding another layer of intimacy to their day.

"They loved me in their own way. I've learned to live with that." She watched the frown on his forehead deepen. His mouth was a thin wary line, yet there was a compassionate glow in his dark eyes. She found herself laughing softly, attempting to lighten the mood. "Goodness. My childhood is nothing worth getting upset over. People do mature. They outgrow wishes scrawled in crayon, Nick."

"I can't help feeling upset about it. But you're right. The past is the past." He kissed the edge of her mouth, then brushed his lips over hers. "What about now? Have you started a wish list for this Christmas, Holly? A mature list?"

"Yes," she choked out. "I want to share the day with you and Emmett, Nick, to share all this colorful heritage you've talked about—"

"Then I hope you're crazy about Yule logs and stuffed cabbage and growing miniature wheat fields on windowsills." He pulled a tendril of hair from beneath her hat and wrapped it around his finger.

His mood had shifted. He was smiling that magical smile she'd grown to anticipate. And the moment was made more wonderful by the scent of pine, the caress of the tree boughs, the feel of Nick's strong arms.

"Did I mention the lighting of the first fire, or the drawing of the first water? Holly, we're talking major ethnic event here. I promise you, it's not for the weak of heart."

Weak of heart? His final words stirred something inside her, a connection so intense she felt a need to step back, out of his arms.

"There's nothing weak about the way I feel toward you, Nick," she said quietly, smiling as his eyes widened in response.

"Holly—"

"Please don't talk, Nick."

"I just wanted to say," he whispered, gesturing with his finger, "there's a deer standing right behind you, one row over. I better warn you, it seems to have an attitude."

* * *

"My father carved this ornament for me when I was just a boy." Emmett pulled a tiny wooden shoe out of the box of tissue-wrapped treasures at his feet. "Why don't we hang the shoes up there next to the miniature wooden skates?"

Nick was careful not to disturb any of Emmett's heirloom glass ornaments hanging on the lower branches as he climbed the ladder and hung the shoe on an upper bough. He turned and from his vantage point he watched Holly take another bourbon ball off the ninety-proof dessert tray.

When they arrived at Emmett's home with the Christmas tree their adoptee had "supper" waiting— a light vegetable soup, hot mulled wine and an assortment of tiny rum-soaked cakes, bourbon balls and strawberries filled with orange liqueur, all courtesy of the neighborhood deli. While Emmett limited himself to soup, Holly and Nick had assuaged their hungry appetites by almost demolishing the tray of delectables.

"Feeling tipsy yet?" Nick asked Holly. "Those bourbon balls can pack a wallop."

"I don't feel a thing. Maybe I have a hollow leg," she teased back, turning in a graceful circle in the center of the living room. She'd changed into a long flowing skirt and a red-and-white sweater after their trek to the woods. The full red skirt swirled as she took a second spin, and Nick smiled as he thought of the Croatian *kolo* dances back in Chicago.

Even without the spirituous dessert tray, the trimming of the tree had been a festive event. Baroque Christmas music and the warm light from the fireplace added to the feeling of celebration.

"That's the last of the ornaments," Emmett announced twenty minutes later. "What we need now is a star. I told you I broke mine years ago—"

"I bought a new one for you, Emmett," Nick announced. "Look in the white box on the end of the coffee table."

"And I made one for you," Holly countered, lifting a tissue-wrapped package from the mantel.

"Hell's bells," Emmett sputtered, scowling first at Nick, then Holly. "Can't you two stop getting your wires crossed? This is as bad as the day you showed up with two turkeys." He shook his head, then motioned both of them to approach. "Well, we better have a look at both of 'em and figure out how to solve this thing."

Nick looked over at Holly. Lord, no. Had he done it again? Stolen her thunder, demeaned her simple homemade offering? He edged toward Emmett feeling like a rat.

"This here's the one Nick bought," Emmett grumbled as he grabbed the white box from the end of the coffee table and removed the lid. Nick could hear Emmett's raspy intake of breath as the older man picked up the shimmering gold-plated star. Inset in the center was an original hologram by a noted Portland artist depicting the earth as seen from space.

"Heavens!" Emmett turned the star back and forth in his hands, his fascination with the three-dimensional image obvious. "How did they do that? There's a little world in there."

"Holly?" Nick saw the hesitancy in her expressive features.

"My star is homemade, Emmett." Her tone was apologetic as she handed the package to their adoptee.

He put the gold star back in the box, his gaze lingering on the hologram for a moment. Then with careful movements, he unwrapped Holly's gift. She'd made a five-point star covered with a flat, shiny sheet of tinsel. As Emmett held the star up, it twirled slightly, catching the warm glow of the flames from the fireplace.

"I admit it's simple, Holly." Emmett tilted his head and watched the star spin. "But she's a beauty. In fact, this little star looks a lot like the ones my mother made for the poor. She did volunteer work, you know."

His well-intentioned remark was followed by an embarrassed silence.

"Thank you, Emmett, but I won't force you to make a decision." Holly took the star from him and bent to pick up the scattered tissue paper.

"He won't have to make a decision. Give me the star of tinsel, Holly." Nick stood next to the Christmas tree, his hands on his hips.

Holly straightened and studied the imposing form of Nick Petrovich. He'd removed the sweater he'd worn to the tree farm and was dressed in a white oxford shirt and narrow red suspenders. His gaze captured and held her as he reached out his hand.

With the trimmed and brightly lit Christmas tree as a backdrop, he seemed another holiday illusion—a man to make the coming weeks complete for her.

Holly held out the homemade star. Nick's fingers brushed hers as he accepted it. As he lifted his hand, letting the star spin from its string, little flashes of reflected firelight danced in the depths of his eyes.

"It's beautiful, Holly. Made of love." With those words, he climbed the ladder and placed the star atop the tree. Two steps down and he was beside her again, taking her in his arms. "Don't forget to make a wish," Nick whispered. "I made mine this afternoon."

"It's past my bedtime!" Emmett's proclamation kept Holly from responding. "If you two don't mind, I'm keeping the gold star in my bedroom." He picked up the gift box.

"Wait!" Holly said and insisted upon testing his blood sugar before he left. Nick used the short interlude to carry the empty boxes that had held ornaments and tree lights up to the attic. When Emmett was settled, Holly returned to the living room to find Nick bent over the fire.

Guitar music was playing, adding to the ambience of warm light and faded festivity. She walked over to the old-fashioned phonograph to straighten the pile of records they'd listened to that evening.

"Just a moment," Nick called out, moving toward her. His step was self-confident, and his eyes sparkled with a mischievous glow. He held out his hand to her and smiled. "I thought it might be nice to end this special night with a little waltz around the room."

There was no time to take his hand. His arm moved round her waist, and Holly found herself drawn against Nick's solid chest. The room became a flurry of colored lights, shimmering ornaments and firelit walls as he led her in an exuberant but graceful waltz around the huge Oriental rug.

Dance after dance, they circled and swirled, caught in a maelstrom of emotion and desire. When the music stopped, Nick gave her one final spin, then drew her back into his arms. After a long moment he raised her palm to his mouth and kissed the sensitive skin.

"I want you, Holly," he whispered, his words a warm wind against the hollow of her hand, fueling the spark of desire that had been burning in her all evening. "I wish I could dance you to the edge of this rug and find us both standing in my bedroom, but I'm afraid that's not possible. There's a small matter of several miles separating where we are and where I believe we both want to be."

Was the warmth that flowed through her love, or should she blame the bourbon balls? Holly wondered, feeling enmeshed in a net of security and warmth, a world of wishes come true.

So little needed to be said. Holly checked on Emmett and turned off the Christmas tree, while Nick banked the fire. He held out her jacket. As she slipped into it, he kissed her neck. "If I recall, I'm the designated driver tonight. Any argument?"

"None," Holly murmured as she handed Nick the keys to the minivan.

Eight

———

During the quick drive to his condo and the short elevator ride to his floor, Nick prayed the magic of the evening would not diminish. He kept the lights dimmed as he led Holly into his large living room.

He studied her awed expression as she took in the panoramic view of the Willamette River, a shimmering ribbon of silver dividing the sparkling lights of downtown Portland and the city's east side. His windows reached from floor to ceiling, but offered the luxury of seeing without being seen.

When she turned to speak, her mouth open, lips half-parted, he heard nothing, only sensed the rush of his own desire.

"Nick, your view—" Holly stammered.

"Hush." He picked up her hands and kissed each palm before resting them against his chest. "My view can't compare to your beauty, Holly. And I'm twice blessed; there's no glass between us. In a few minutes nothing will separate us."

"I'd like that." She wrapped her hands around the straps of his suspenders, sliding up and down his chest, her knuckles creating a delicious friction between the fabric of his shirt and his nipples.

Raising his hand, Nick touched a fingertip to the top button of Holly's V-necked cardigan. The smooth bone buttons gave easily as did the buttons on the blouse beneath. In moments the flowing red skirt joined the blouse and sweater on the floor, and she stood before him wearing only a pink satin teddy edged in lace. In the subdued lighting shadows hid the rise of her breasts, shadows he longed to explore.

"You're even more beautiful than I imagined," he said in a hoarse whisper, "and my imagination has been running wild all day."

She moaned as his hands moved downward and he brushed the outer curve of her breasts with his palms. The silk slithered beneath his touch as he stroked his thumbs across the hardened buds at the crest of her curves.

Nick was only vaguely aware of the movement of her hands until he felt her breath against the bare flesh of his chest. She'd unbuttoned his shirt and was spreading her fingers across his midriff.

"I'm fascinated with your suspenders, but I'll have to take them off if I want to see all of you, Mr. Petrovich." Her words inflamed him as much as her movements. She teased the narrow red straps from his shoulders and coaxed his shirt over his arms, forcing him to pause in his exploration.

She pulled his shirttails from his jeans as he looked at her with a mixture of surprise and passion. With a smile, she held up his shirt and tossed it into the air. The white fabric fluttered to the rug like a flag of surrender, but Holly knew there was no defeat. They had both given way to their mutual desire hours ago, while surrounded by the scent of pine, embracing in a field of holiday splendor. Nirvana Tree Farm had been a prophetic choice.

With Nick's upper torso open to the warmth of her appreciative gaze, she let her hands slip downward to his belt buckle.

"Let me," he offered, reaching toward his waist.

"But this is half of my pleasure," she protested.

"At the moment it's my torment," Nick corrected.

Reluctantly she let him take the lead, knowing there'd be another time when she would insist on undressing him slowly, with teasing touches and languid strokes of her tongue. She would learn to pleasure him and teach him what pleasured her. But tonight their passion was unleashed, and they were unwilling to wait.

When Nick stepped out of his jeans, he was wearing only narrow black briefs. Scandalously brief.

He observed Holly's reaction with a chuckle. "And they say women don't react to visual stimuli as strongly as men. I'd say we're even in that department. I love this wispy little thing you're wearing." His fingers brushed the tiny satin straps of her teddy from her shoulders. The bodice fell in a silken whisper to her waist.

But his eyes remained locked with hers. With gentle movements he pulled the fabric over her hips. She was naked, open to his scrutiny, but Nick continued to focus on her face, giving her that mysterious, knowing smile. She felt warmed by the inner fire she found in the depths of his eyes. Her nipples tightened with hunger for his touch, for all of him.

"Nick," Holly whispered, taking his hands, pressing them to her breasts. He tested their weight in his palms, brushing the dusky rose tips with his thumbs until she moaned and moved against him.

Nick lowered Holly to the sea of pillows in a corner of his living room.

Holly's fingers stroked him through the black briefs. He took a deep breath of anticipation as she edged the fabric down. Nick shuddered with rocketing sensations when Holly's fingers curled around him, stroking and caressing him with the soft, clinging warmth of her hand.

Holly felt her own waves of desire at knowing she had aroused Nick to such a state. She studied the whole man with her eyes—the broad shoulders, the firmly muscled midriff and the slim hips—while her hand explored the silk and steel of his heavy arousal. No questions lingered in her mind as they had earlier in the day. Her hand moved over his hip to caress the firm rounded flesh of his buttocks, to urge his body closer.

The faint smell of pine wafted from him. It was still in his hair, on his skin, a reminder of their day of sharing. The warmth that had gathered in her chest all afternoon and evening became a bright ember fueled further by the memory of Nick's hand reaching for the star of tinsel.

Her fingers caught in his hair as he brought his mouth down to her breast and lightly touched a swollen tip with rhythmic, flicking motions of his tongue.

He drew her into his mouth, gradually expanding the circles his tongue made until Holly closed her eyes against the exquisite sensation. Flashes of light played against her eyelids, and her heartbeat seemed to pulse wherever Nick moved his tongue.

His nails raked gently over her abdomen, his fingers taking her with a slow intimate possession. When she tightened her muscles at the pleasurable feeling, he relaxed his movements only to begin again.

The ripples of pleasure turned to unbearable tremors. Holly's breath became ragged, and fifty phantom pulses seemed to beat an erratic rhythm that pulled her toward Nick and away from him at the same time. She flushed as a desperate cry escaped her throat.

Nick muffled her small, ragged gasps with his mouth.

"Love me, Nick," she pleaded in a voice she hardly recognized.

His fingers entered her again, gauging her readiness. "Not until you're ready for me." The tip of his tongue caught the edge of her mouth, outlining the fullness of her lips before plunging deep inside and tasting the liquid warmth. "I don't want to hurt you, Holly."

He moved lower, leaving a trail of glistening moisture from the edge of her delicate jawline to the scented valley between her breasts.

He paid homage to her perfection with his hands and mouth, with words whispered into the hollow of her throat, against the silken sweep of her thighs.

Not trusting the vestige of control that remained, Nick splayed his fingers against Holly's narrow waist and urged her to move over him.

She watched the loving message in his dark, expressive eyes as she hovered above him. Trembling, she lowered herself to accept the throbbing pressure that brought a flare of renewed pleasure.

With each measured thrust the chaotic rhythm of desire that had built all day evolved into a harmonious blending of male and female, uniting them in oneness.

Holly opened her eyes as her pleasure peaked and spiraled. The panoramic lights of the city blurred and melded with the myriad of sensations she felt helpless to control.

Nick's strong arms pulled her down against him as he shuddered with his own release. Afterward they lay a heartbeat apart, and she felt her eyes grow moist from the beauty and completeness of their loving.

Long moments later she heard Nick murmur softly to her, then felt the gentle motion of his arms lifting her, carrying her. She stirred again when he settled her against cool sheets.

"Good night, love," he whispered, tucking her into the warm curve of his body.

Holly stood at one of the floor-to-ceiling windows sipping coffee, the special gourmet-blend cold-drip concentrate that Nick had made to order and picked up from a local shop twice a week. It tasted slightly bitter on her tongue. She moved to the next glass panel as she took in Nick's view of Portland. If only it were this easy to get a better perspective of her feelings.

The day had started in afterglow. She'd opened her eyes to find Nick touching her hair, smiling down at her.

"You hiccuped," he accused, lowering his head to the pillow and speaking into the sleepy warmth between them. "Just once. Like a baby after a long cry."

What did he know about babies? "Liar," she mumbled into the hollow between his neck and shoulder.

"You're probably a little hung over from bourbon balls and rum cakes. It's a good thing I'm here." His hand coaxed the comforter from her shoulder. "I know a sure cure."

The cure was purely physical. They made love again, tender, unhurried love.

As their breathing slowed to normal and morning light illuminated the details of his bedroom, Holly felt an uneasy ache in her stomach. The bedroom was a sterile blend of black lacquered furniture in bold art-deco designs and scarlet linens and accents. Two erotic line drawings hung near the bed, but it was the neon half-moon in the corner that caught her eye. Nick had a manufactured moon in his bedroom.

They showered together, exploring one another's bodies anew. As Nick dried her back with a large towel, she took in the details of the high-tech black-and-white bathroom. The uneasy ache in Holly's stomach became a knot. Like the bedroom, the bathroom decor was sleek, beautiful, tasteful, but was it Nick? Or was there another side to the man, a side she had yet to explore?

She pondered the same question after seeing the living room and kitchen. Clean, geometric lines and wild splashes of color. The rooms could have belonged to anyone. There was no sense of having been lived in—none of the warmth and masculine, old-world charm that she associated with Nick Petrovich.

He approached the window and took the empty coffee cup from her hand. "Why don't I show you my work area?"

He led her down the hall to a room filled with computers, printers and some machines she failed to recognize. The awards displayed on one wall were obscured by the blueprints and computer printouts dangling from wires suspended from the ceiling. The outer walls were covered with signed posters of ultra-modern building designs.

"A bit chaotic, isn't it?" Nick asked.

"No, even in here there's an order to the chaos," she stammered as she searched for the correct response. They were beyond that point now, the need to be correct, precise, polite. She wanted to be honest with him.

"I'm sorry, Nick, but in all the rooms I've seen I don't get a real sense of *you*. Who you are. Your hates, your loves, your, your passions. Your immigrant roots."

"My immigrant roots?" Nick exclaimed.

Holly knew she'd been quiet, noncommittal in her comments about his decor, but he must have sensed her displeasure.

"What did you expect to find here?" he asked, frowning slightly.

Holly leaned against the doorjamb. "A reflection of you, Nick. This and everything else—" she took the room in with a sweep of her hand "—it surprised me. Everything is beautiful, crisp, sweeping, high-tech, but it's a bit sterile, almost cold. In my eyes, you're not like that. But that's not all—"

"Holly—"

"Seeing this room reminds me that you work primarily alone. At the salon I work with people one-on-one, touching them, listening to their problems. It's rewarding."

"I find my work rewarding, too, Holly."

"I believe that, but I have problems getting involved with a man with priorities so different from my own. I need to be assured your ambition doesn't interfere with enjoying the simple things in life."

"Maybe I should explain something." Nick grabbed his drafting chair and turned it around. He resented her conclusions, but felt the need to plead his case. "Designing computer programs for architects is the career I've chosen for myself, but I'm not doing it for the money. I enjoy this work. It's an integral part of my life."

He sat facing her, his arms resting across the back of the chair, his robe opening to display a fair amount of thigh. "In fact, I'm regarded as something of an expert on the subject of modern architecture. I write articles, work with people in the field."

"I respect that—"

"No, you don't," he challenged her. "Not when you expect to see my immigrant roots hanging on these walls or woven into a quilt covering my bed. Did you expect me to dress in *nošnja*, my national costume, this morning and serve you *politza*, a cake of nuts and honey, for breakfast?"

"Nick! I'm not talking about turning your home into a shrine to nationalistic pride. I'm talking about self-expression. I don't see the inner man, your warmth and sensitivity." She shook her head and threw up her hands.

"I don't know," she added. "Maybe there's more to it. Look at how we've been interacting for the past month. I'm used to meeting you at Emmett's house. There's the fireplace and cozy furniture and a certain intimacy. It was probably wrong of me to expect to feel that way here. Maybe, Nick, maybe I don't really know you."

Holly turned and stalked down the hall, embarrassed by her outburst and lack of subtlety. She fumbled unsuccessfully with the knot in the belt of the spare bathrobe Nick had given her after their shower. As she walked into the living room, she began searching for the clothes she'd worn last night.

Nick's hands grasped her upper arms and turned her around. "Please don't ever walk away from me when you're angry," he said firmly. "Give me a chance to explain my feelings. It's not easy, especially when I've never put them into words before." He embraced her gently, holding her loosely against his chest. "And you do know me, far better than you realize, Holly. Trust your instincts. For God's sake, don't let the decor of my home change your impression of me."

He took a deep breath. "Just try to understand, a man doesn't have to put his heritage on display. My roots are in here, Holly." He pulled back and held a hand against his heart. "They're in my name and written in my features." He picked up her hand and kissed it, then touched her fingers to the bridge of his nose. "My father's nose." Nick moved her hand outward. "The high cheekbones from my mother's family."

"And the eyes?" She released her hand and traced the arch of his eyebrows, touching a fingertip to the long lashes that framed his magnetic brown eyes.

"My paternal grandfather, they say. The guy must have been part cocker spaniel."

"My favorite breed," she said softly.

He smiled warmly in response, and she moved her finger to his mouth to trace the firm curve of his lower lip.

"Come with me," he whispered, taking her hand in his. He urged her to follow him into the bedroom. "Sit down on the bed. I want to show you something."

From the far recesses of his closet he brought out his velvet-draped *tamburitza* and unwrapped the instrument.

"Nick?" Holly reached out to touch the strings. "What—this looks a little bit like a mandolin. What is it?"

He sat on the bed beside her and began to strum it. "*Tamburitza*. It's a popular instrument in Croatian communities. Goes back about thirteen centuries, give or take a year."

Nick eased into a simple folk tune that he'd learned from his father.

"Sometimes I feel torn." He spoke softly as he played. "I want to think of myself as a man of the eighties, but I'll be straightforward. I find myself struggling with the traditionalist within. The roots run deep, Holly, and what you said a little while ago touched that part of me."

"Nick, I'm sorry. I had no right to spout off like that about priorities and life-style—"

"No, it's all right. Let me finish, Holly." He looked down at the instrument, amazed that his fingers moved so easily over the strings. "There was a time in my childhood when I felt special. I was Croatian. I knew my parents were from Yugoslavia, and I heard the relatives talk about the old country with reverence and sometimes with pain. But as I got older, I realized my accent and funny customs and poverty set me apart from other kids at school. I vowed to change my immigrant image, to become a successful, sophisticated man, but at the same time, I vowed to retain the pride I felt for my roots."

"And you've done that, Nick."

"No, I haven't. I used to think I'd honored both vows. I told you before I hurt my parents last Christmas by making fun of the old ways. This year, I'm celebrating without them. I'm trying to hold on to the traditions, and I'm discovering how much they mean to me—because of you, Holly."

"What have I done?"

"A lot of different things, I guess. I've never felt this close to a woman before, free enough to play my *tamburitza*." He plucked out the opening notes of a Croatian love ballad his father and uncles often played at weddings.

"Maybe it's simply a matter of trust." She leaned her head on his shoulder.

No, Holly, it's a matter of listening, caring, loving, Nick thought, but he wasn't ready to commit himself, to put labels on the emotions warring within. Could she honestly believe his ambition outweighed his human qualities?

He concentrated on the love song for a moment, hoping the music would convey his feelings.

He spoke after a few minutes. "I was thinking about this Christmas, Holly. Wouldn't it be nice if we could plan a special surprise for Emmett? With your mandolin and my *tamburitza*, we could play a duet."

"That's a great idea."

"There's one Christmas song that's special to me. It's Croatian. I'd love to teach it to you."

"And I'd love to learn it."

They talked for awhile about their musical backgrounds and preferences.

"We'll need to practice a bit, but I think we'll be good together, Holly."

"We *are* good together." She reached over to strum the *tamburitza* in his lap. "We found that out last night and again this morning," Holly whispered, slipping her hand inside his robe to stroke his upper thigh. "I don't know what you're playing, Nick, but it's making me think about harmony. Perhaps we should begin practicing our fingering patterns immediately."

"No fair." He set the instrument down and took her into his arms. "You're way ahead of me."

Nine

"Anyone here?" Holly walked into Emmett's kitchen, brushing snowflakes from her hair and jacket.

"Save me, Holly. Please!" Emmett gasped from the darkened pantry.

"What are you doing—"

"Hush! Don't let him know I'm in here," her adoptee whispered.

Holly glanced around the kitchen. "Let who know?"

"Nick. Who else?" Emmett's eyes widened emphatically as he motioned Holly through the pantry door.

"I don't understand. I just got here. The snow has traffic snarled." She closed the door behind her and turned on the overhead light. "Why are you hiding from Nick?"

"He's changed, Holly. Somethin's happened to him during the past few days."

Holly felt partly responsible for the change in Nick. He'd been acting differently ever since their weekend together. But it was a wonderful kind of different.

"I'm a little surprised. I thought you liked the changes, Emmett."

"He's a volunteer, Holly. I didn't want to hurt his feelings. You know I studied acting years ago. I feel like I've earned an Oscar these past few days." Emmett toyed with the latch on one of the antiquated cupboard doors.

"What has he done that's bothered you?"

"I hate to sound ungrateful. The two of you have really brightened my life but—" Emmett searched her eyes "—I asked Nick to rent some video tapes, and instead, the durn fool goes to the library and checks out Dickens and Tolstoy and insists on readin' to me!"

"I thought he explained that to you. Nick thought you were becoming addicted to cable TV and the VCR, Emmett," Holly reiterated. "He wanted to read to you, share a little human interaction."

"The man can save his breath. They've got books on tape these days! And everyone knows Hollywood's made movies of all the classics. If I have to sit there and listen to him drone on about 'These were the best of times, they were the worst of times'—oh, Lord." Emmett threw up his hands. "Me, I'm just interested in having a *good* time. I keep falling asleep when Nick reads."

But I don't. Holly recalled the evening Nick had continued reading after Emmett had begun to snore softly. He had a marvelous voice, deep, rich, vibrant. She'd put down her crafts project and nestled beside him on the love seat, looking up now and then with approving glances to let him know she was listening intently.

Emmett lowered his voice back down to a faint whisper. "What happened to the old Nick?"

"Emmett, this might be my fault," Holly said with a sigh. She turned to the shelf of spices. For lack of anything better to do, she began arranging them in alphabetical order. "You see, last weekend, during an emotional moment, I said something about men who let ambition interfere with their ability to appreciate the simple things in life. I think Nick took my comment to heart. He's trying to approach you on a more personal level." She found the allspice and moved it to the top of the shelf. "You know, share life's simple joys."

"What the hell for? I didn't mind the presents! Wait till you see what he brought over today. A miniature field of wheat growin' in a bowl. One of his Croatian Christmas customs, he says. How am I supposed to act excited about putting wheat in my windowsill and waking up Christmas mornin' and sticking a fool candle in it?"

"Let's see, basil and bay leaves." Holly continued her sorting. "I'm sure there's a lot of symbolism involved in wheat that he'll explain later. We have to respect other people's traditions, Emmett." She recalled Nick mentioning a miniature wheat field, but she was as perplexed as the older man. "Where is he now? Why are we hiding in the pantry?"

"He might be out in the garage, or he could be down in the basement fussing on that surprise project."

"Surprise project? He didn't mention anything to me."

"Of course not. That's why it's a surprise, girl. We're not supposed to know the details. He's been making a fair amount of noise down in the basement and won't let me take a look. That's another part of the change in him. He's gotten sneaky."

"He's always been sneaky." Holly searched for the spices beginning with *C*. Chili powder. Coriander. "Come on, why don't we stop whispering and open the door. Try to understand that he's making an effort not to be so extravagant. He's offering the gift of—"

"No, wait! I didn't tell you everything." Emmett blocked the doorway. "Nick insists on learning how to test my blood sugar."

"I'm impressed. Why are you worried?"

"Don't you remember the way he butchered our Thanksgiving turkeys?"

"Hmm, that was a rather tense day, remember? He's a very gentle man. Don't worry. He won't treat you like a turkey, Emmett." *Unless you keep acting like one.*

"How do you know? Has he taken blood from *your* finger?"

"Well, no, but I'm very...observant," Holly stammered. She'd spent more than her share of time at Nick's condo this week. He was a passionate, sometimes demanding lover, but he was always gentle, sensitive and caring.

"I can't stand it, Holly. What are we going to do about Nick?" Emmett gestured with a jar of spice.

She was repeating Emmett's question when the door to the pantry swung open.

"Holly! Emmett! I thought I heard voices. Emmett, I've been looking all over for you." Nick stepped back, his imposing form almost filling the doorway. "What are you two doing in here?"

"Uhh, helpin' Holly put these spices back into alphabetical order. Here's that cinnamon. Let's see, what else starts with the letter *C*?"

"Cardamom. Cayenne." Nick cast an accusing glance at Holly. He'd overheard her last comment. "Cloakroom. Conspiracy."

"I'm going outside to check for mail," Emmett mumbled quickly as he edged past Nick.

"Chameleon. Collusion. Caught in the act," Nick added for good measure as he stepped inside the pantry.

"Celery seed, chives, cloves." Holly continued sorting the spices. "We weren't plotting against you, Nick. It's not what you think." She looked up at him and laughed. "In fact, the truth is kind of funny."

"Confess." Nick moved behind her, lowering his head to kiss the lobe of her ear. "Conniving cosmetologist."

"Crabby Croatian." She turned and he captured her in his embrace.

"Enough alliteration." Touching her chin, Nick raised her face until her gaze met his. He was struck again by the impact of her dove-gray eyes and rich auburn waves. Was she growing more beautiful daily? He'd prided himself on being analytical in his work, but when it came to Holly the romantic in him took over.

The room was filled with the smells and colors of an alphabet of spices, and yet he could only focus on the faint scent of her perfume and hair the color of cayenne pepper.

"So I imagined overhearing you ask him 'What are we going to do about Nick?' Mind telling me what's going on here?"

"Okay." Holly bit her lower lip.

The sight of her even white teeth pressing against the sensual fullness of her lower lip distracted him further. That mouth had pleasured him, those teeth... Nick forced himself to listen.

"Emmett thinks you've changed, Nick. He doesn't like being read to, and he said something about a bowl of wheat."

"Poor guy. Maybe I'm overdoing the human interaction." Nick ran his fingers through the snow-dampened waves near her face. "I still don't understand why Emmett gets a kick out of the home-crafted gifts and haircuts you give him, but he expects something else from me."

"Think back. Haven't you spoiled him all along? He's come to depend on it." Holly reached up and brushed Nick's hair back from his forehead. Her hand returned to rest on the side of his face. She ran her thumb back and forth over the high arch of his cheekbone. "By the way, he's also afraid to let you test his blood sugar."

"I just want to learn the basics." He turned his head to kiss her palm as he drew her closer. "There are times when you're not here, and if he was in trouble, I'd want to know how to help."

"I'll teach you. We'll practice with *your* fingers."

"Thanks." He leaned his forehead against hers. "Can I ask you a question, Holly?"

"Anytime."

"Just what do you consider the simple things in life?"

"Hmm, kissing in the pantry for starters."

As his lips touched her, he felt the vibration of her laughter against his mouth. Nick pulled back.

"Simple things, huh?" He stroked her lower lip with his thumb, then replaced his finger with the firm fullness of his mouth. "What ever made you think I wouldn't appreciate anything as wonderful as this? Or this?" His lips moved against hers until he felt himself losing control. "Let's close the door. You can be the maid, and I'll be the lusty butler."

"Whoa!" She stepped back, laughing. "We can play house tonight, but right now I want to talk about last weekend. I wish you hadn't taken my comments so seriously."

"I figured you wouldn't have said it if there wasn't substance to the thought. You're not the one who's upset, it's Emmett."

"Well, yes, you're right about that."

"Now, I have a surprise for you and Emmett. It's out in the garage. Why don't we find the frightened Mr. Snow, weatherproof ourselves and have a look? I promise not to read aloud or take blood samples."

"Sounds intriguing. I can't wait. One last thing." Holly glanced over her shoulder at the shelf. "Is cocoa a spice?"

"I don't know." Nick smiled as he took the can from her and placed it on the ledge. "I have a question for you, Holly, about words starting with *C*."

He lowered his voice. "Is cherish the same thing as love? Because that's the way I feel about you." He touched a finger to her cheek. Her mouth was parted in surprise, her eyes questioning. Did she realize how strong his feelings were? He took her hand and moved toward the pantry door. He didn't really expect an answer to his question . . . until Christmas.

"Here comes a monster mogul!" Nick shouted from his position behind Holly on the sled. His arms tightened around her waist as they hit the ridge of closely packed snow in front of Emmett's house at full speed.

Holly strained as she shifted her feet on the steering bar and grasped the rope tautly, squinting against the falling snow to steer the sled away from the next bone-jarring bump.

"Left. Left. Let's go for it!" Nick shouted. Using his weight advantage, he overrode her attempts to stabilize the sled and steered it directly up to the next ridge. "Hyperspace!"

Holly felt a scream lodge in her throat as the sled became airborne. She gave up any effort to control their path.

An afternoon of sledding had shown Holly a different side of Nick. He was a daredevil—a reckless, certifiable, risk-taking fool when it came to steep hills and a pre-Christmas snowfall. He'd found Emmett's childhood sled in the garage and invested a few clandestine hours scraping, cleaning and oiling the *Flexible Flyer*, giving the wooden toy a second life.

And now endangering hers!

Closing her eyes, she leaned back against Nick's solid chest and lost herself in a flurry of exhilarating speed and weightlessness.

The impact of the sled hitting the snow-covered pavement jarred her into full alert. The bottom of the hill was rapidly approaching, and Nick gave no hint of slowing down.

"I'm going to test the brakes!" he shouted.

"We don't have brakes!" Holly screamed back.

"Oh yes, we do!" He dug his heels into the snow and performed an audacious U-turn after teetering on the crest of the next hill. The force sent them sprawling into the snow and flipped the sled upside down.

Holly lay spread-eagled on her back, staring up at the huge flakes of falling snow and wondering why she had left the comfort of the pantry—the smell of spices and the warmth of Nick's mouth on hers. She was vaguely aware of Emmett's cheer from the front yard.

"Best run yet, wasn't it?" Nick was suddenly hovering over her. "Emmett seems to agree." His dark hair was tousled in a boyish manner, snow-dampened curls stuck to his forehead and temple, and his brown eyes shone with excitement. His arm curved around her waist as he moved beside her.

They lay in the snow, but Holly felt no cold, only the heat of his gaze. For an instant, the cocoon of intimacy they'd found in the pantry returned, and she thought of their conversation. Cherish. The use of the word added to Nick's old-world charm.

Love. Cherish. Where lay the difference? There had been two men in her life who'd used the word love. Both had used it early in what turned out to be short-term relationships and with a casual ease that bothered Holly. Had anyone ever cherished her? Why now? Why Nick?

"You're a good sport, Holly." He cuffed her chin lightly with his gloved knuckles.

Was it normal, she wondered, for a man to test the endurance and endanger the life of the woman he cherished and chalk it up to good sportsmanship?

"If you don't mind sitting on the sidelines for a little while, Holly," he said quickly without showing any sign of exertion, "I'd like to take Emmett for a couple of runs."

"He'll have a cardiac arrest!"

"Emmett? Sledding is no worse than riding the Matterhorn at Disneyland." Nick chuckled as he got to his feet and brushed clumps of snow from the runners and slats on the sled. "He'll love it. He's a man of adventure. Fearless, brave, plucky." Nick picked up the *Flexible Flyer* and started walking with her back up the hill. "Just like you."

"Look at him." Holly nodded toward the lone figure in front of the house halfway up the slope. "Your Captain Courageous has spent the last hour constructing a snow woman in his front yard. Don't pressure him into doing anything reckless, Nick."

"Aren't you the one who said he didn't get out of the house enough? He has to perform a few deeds of derring-do, flex those muscles—"

"And you think he should do that on a vintage sled?"

"Why not? Sounds like a 'simple pleasure' to me." Nick gave her one of those mysterious smiles, made all the more intriguing by his boyishly disheveled hair and the high color in his cheeks.

"Are you trying to make up for that wholesome image you've been projecting all week by showing Emmett you're willing to take chances?"

"No." Nick held up a gloved finger. "I'm trying to give him a chance to find his own inner strength. Please observe."

Their adoptee was thoroughly absorbed in the task of building his snow woman.

"Emmett!" Nick called out. "She's lookin' good. Why don't you let Holly work on the makeup and hair while you and I take a couple of runs down the hill together?"

Emmett shielded his eyes from the snow with his hand as he moved with slow deliberate strides toward the path. "You want me to ride on the sled?"

"Of course. Come on. Our steed awaits us." Nick repeated the invitation, beckoning to Emmett with his free hand as he set the sled on the ground.

Emmett cleared his throat awkwardly. "You got seat belts and air bags on this thing?" He kicked the steering bar, then circled the *Flexible Flyer* with halting movements while Nick praised the sled's performance.

"What about collision insurance?" Emmett stuck his lower lip out and frowned at Nick. He appeared to be stalling, adjusting his gloves and checking and rechecking the top button of his thick wool coat.

"You're the original owner, Emmett. You know about these older models. No seat belts or air bags, and they won't give me insurance on it, but we all know older is sometimes better, don't you think?"

"Damn right!" Emmett's expression brightened. He held up his chin. "Where do ya want me? Front or back of this rig?"

"Front." Nick maintained a wide stance in the snow and held the rope firmly in his grasp while Emmett settled on the wooden slats.

"Hey, Nick." His adoptee half turned. "This isn't your way of getting blood out of me without sticking my finger?"

"Now there's an idea." Nick chuckled as he pulled the sled out into the center of the deserted street. Reaching down, he tugged at the older man's stocking cap until it felt secure. "Let's wave goodbye to the womenfolk up on the bank. Wish us luck!" he called.

Holly was standing beside the snow woman, adding the finishing touches to Emmett's creation. She turned, waved and shook the stick that represented the snow woman's arm. "Good luck. I'll be praying for you, Emmett!"

For an instant Nick was struck by the image of Holly standing beside the woman of snow. The private investigator he'd hired had been successful in his efforts to locate Delilah Carpenter. The widow was in good health, living in the suburbs of Los Angeles and in the process of selling the chain of movie theaters she'd run with her late husband. The reunion between Emmett and Delilah now rested on her decision.

If Delilah responded to Nick's letter in time, Holly could be standing beside a flesh-and-blood woman one week from today on Christmas morning.

"Nick." Emmett's voice was trembling. "I'm not real sure about this after all. My stomach's fluttering."

"So is mine," Nick responded. "Butterflies. It's part of taking chances."

"I'm not sure about that. With me, I think it's part of being scared witless. I might get hurt."

"Then I'll keep my feet down on the first run to slow our speed. No bumps, no risk taking. All right?"

"Okay. I trust you, Nick."

"The first run was a slow, uneventful glide.

"Let's do it again," Emmett urged as they walked back up the hill.

"Good luck, again." Holly waved from the bank.

As Nick waved back, Emmett turned.

"I say, Nick." The older man's voice took on a decidedly British air. "The enemy is behind us. We secret agents have no time for goodbyes."

"And your name?" Nick played along as he nosed the sled to the right, preparing for descent.

"Snow. Emmett 'Eat My Dust' Snow. Let's lose 'em!"

Driven by the forceful command, Nick let the sled gain momentum and ran behind it for several yards before jumping on next to Emmett. Nick raised his feet onto the steering bar and guided the sled away from the hazardous ridges, but managed to throw in a couple of fail-safe hairpin turns and an exciting finish.

The sound of Emmett's laughter, almost childlike in its intensity and reflected joy, thrilled Nick. It was a moment of realization. Despite the cantankerous, crusty exterior, he liked this man. A bond had formed between them that couldn't be dictated by volunteer duty. Emmett had just passed a crossroad from passive fear to involvement. He'd accepted a challenge and overcome his uncertainty.

"How'd you like it?" Nick asked as he extended a hand to Emmett.

"On my scale of one to ten for adventure, it rates a solid eight." Breathlessly Emmett suggested they take another run and hit a few of the ridges head-on.

Nick hesitated, searching Emmett's eyes for signs of false bravado. How much was too much? On one hand, he couldn't risk a jarring landing, a possible broken bone. On the other hand, it was just as important to preserve the older man's dignity and masculinity and allow him to explore his newfound strength. Was there a middle ground?

He talked Emmett into taking only a few mild risks on their third run. Again the sound of his adoptee's laughter was contagious.

As he climbed the hill once more, slowing his pace to match Emmett's, he studied the proud profile at his side. What would happen in February when Holly and Nick were no longer involved in the Chain of Caring project? Would Emmett's life seem emptier after tasting the joys of the special relationship?

And what about Nick's relationship with Holly? Their time together had revolved around Emmett Snow, their chosen professions and the stolen evenings of passion spent in his condo.

He'd seen her renovated Victorian only once. They'd practiced their Christmas duet on *tamburitza* and mandolin while lying on her four-poster bed, which had been bathed in winter sunlight diffused through filmy lace curtains.

The women in his life had never understood his irregular work hours or spurts of inspiration, but Holly did. Her own schedule was always changing, and she usually worked a total of three days a week. More and more he found himself arranging his leisure time to coincide with hers.

"Anyone for a cup of hot cocoa?" Holly shouted from the front door as Nick and Emmett climbed the path to the house.

She smiled and laughed as she helped Emmett off with his coat and playfully snatched his stocking cap. Then her thickly lashed eyes lifted, and her gaze met Nick's. In a world of swirling white she was every color, every emotion, everything he'd ever dreamed of in a woman.

"Nick! I've been missing my workout partner. Where've you been?"

Nick looked up from the display case to find the dashing figure of Dr. Mitch Donnely approaching across the plush carpet of Portland's finest jewelry store. Damn. The timing was rotten. He was already having second thoughts about his purchases. The presence of a twice-divorced, confirmed bachelor was the last thing he needed.

"Mitch." Nick greeted his friend in a subdued tone befitting the solemn ambience of the elegant salon. "Sorry I've missed you. I had to rearrange my workout schedule lately."

"Meaning things went well with the redhead and your volunteer tiling project?"

"Yeah, the floor looks great."

"I was more interested in the redhead."

"Her name is Holly, Mitch." Nick looked anxiously at the clerk who'd been waiting on him. "I'll just say the relationship is moving along nicely."

"Which translates into please don't knock on my door and borrow any sugar for the next few months, right?"

The female clerk set the charge slip on the counter and handed Nick a pen. "If you'd just sign this, Mr. Petrovich. We're wrapping your packages now. It'll be a few minutes."

Nick bent down to sign the charge slip.

"So, Nick, have you done a little Christmas shopping for this Holly?" Mitch tried glancing over Nick's shoulder, but Nick artfully adjusted his stance. Undeterred, Mitch waited until the clerk returned to the register. "Exactly what did you buy her?"

"A little jewelry. She's very special to me." *Disappear!* Nick wanted to shout. *This is private and personal, and I'm already unnerved by the whole experience.* "What are you in here for?"

"I'm having a diamond replaced in my watch. So, how serious is this thing with your fellow volunteer?"

"Speaking of volunteerism, Dr. Donnely." Nick steered the conversation away from Holly. "I told you about the older man we're spending time with. He's a diabetic on oral medication, but he's having some problems with fluctuation of his blood sugar. I want to pick out one of those electronic monitors—"

"How's his eyesight?"

"He's mentioned that it's failing."

"Then I'd recommend one of the new audible readout meters. The blood sugar is read aloud by an electronic voice. In fact, I know a supply place over by Sandy Boulevard. We can drive over there now, and I'll help you pick one out. You'll need some supplies to go with it and instructions on how to use it."

"No, I can't impose on you like that."

"It's no problem," Mitch countered. "I've felt a little guilty ever since you started this volunteer thing. I've been thinking I should get involved with a project. Until then, let me do this much."

"You really have the time, Mitch? I have a thousand questions to ask about Emmett's condition."

"Actually, I'd love to help. Let me get this diamond replaced, and I'll be right with you."

"Terrific." After Nick watched Mitch walk to the other side of the salon, he stepped to the end of the counter. "Are my packages ready yet?"

"Here they are, Mr. Petrovich." The young woman smiled and indicated two gift-wrapped boxes on the counter. "The necklace—" she pointed to the larger box "—and the ring." As she slipped them into a gold brocade sack, she looked up at Nick and frowned. "You still seem a little uncertain, sir."

He shrugged. "I guess the holidays do funny things to people."

"Yes, they can. If you change your mind about the ring just ask for me by name." Her voice was empathetic. "Your friend may want something more elaborate."

Nick thought of the thin gold band decorated with a wheat pattern broken by the glimmer of recessed diamonds. The design was elegantly simple. The only question left in his mind was the purpose. Was this going to be a friendship ring or an accompaniment to a proposal?

"I don't think there'll be a problem," he said quietly.

Ten

Sorry. Maybe unnatural wasn't the best choice of words.'' Sara Tanaka leaned against the doorjamb of the treatment room where Holly was cleansing a client's face, one of the first steps before a total make-over. "But I can't think of another term to describe the way you'll be spending Christmas. I'm just so used to being with family, and you know, we have these established traditions—oh boy, would you listen to me. I'm making it worse, right? First the foot in the mouth, now the—"

"Sara, it's all right. Really." Holly noted the hand signals of her client and adjusted the micro head-phones that piped in the salon's subliminal relaxation tape.

"I'm not judging what you're doing," Sara added. "I just have a different perspective."

"I understand. For you, family is everything. In your eyes I'm spending Christmas with near strangers." Holly began rinsing off the cleanser. Secretly she wished her longtime friend and coworker could accept the fact that she was happy about the Chain of Caring project and the way things had turned out for the holidays.

"Look, I don't want you to think I'm beating a dead horse—"

"A dead reindeer might be more appropriate." Holly interjected as she began the toning and exfoliation process.

Sara groaned. "This is serious. Tomorrow night is Christmas Eve. You have to give this some thought. Look ahead to next year. Nick's parents will be home. He'll return to Chicago to celebrate in his own way, and Emmett Snow might get another volunteer. I hate to see you setting yourself up for a disappointment in the future."

"Disappointment? Sara, I've never had a Christmas that met any of my expectations. Never. Maybe I won't be with family, but then the word family doesn't hold the same meaning for me that it does for you."

Holly lowered the overhead lamp and intently studied the pores of the middle-aged woman in the chair. The past week had been hectic. She'd worked a few twelve-hour days to accommodate all the clients who wanted to look good for the holidays. She inhaled deeply and forced herself to relax.

"Sara, I'd like to think family has nothing to do with blood ties or obligation or heritage. Nick and Emmett and I have become a family of sorts, because we care about each other. We're sharing more than just the holidays. Emmett's like a great-uncle and Nick is..."

Holly searched for the right word as she looked through a shelf of moisturizers.

"I'm your friend, Holly. Why is it so hard for you to use the word lover to describe Nick Petrovich?"

Holly turned to face the dark-haired woman in the doorway. "Last night Nick and I sat in his living room until midnight, fully dressed I might add, practicing a Croatian Christmas carol and other duets to play for Emmett. In the past week we've gone sledding, we took Emmett to Pioneer Square to see the Christmas tree for the second time and over to the Portland Building to see the statue of Portlandia." She grabbed a moisturizer from the shelf, then paused to recheck the label. "Nick and I might be lovers, but there's so much more, Sara. So much."

"*Sre-zic*...how's it go?" Emmett leaned forward.

"Are you sure you didn't drink more than one glass of that champagne?" Nick teased. "Okay. Try it again. *Sretan Božić.*" He pronounced each syllable carefully.

Emmett repeated the phrase slowly. "Hear that, Holly? I'm saying Merry Christmas in Croatian. Lordy, the way things are shaping up this year, we'll be using that phrase a lot."

Holly's soft laughter was lost in the joyous Christmas music emanating from the compact disc player Nick had given Emmett. Nick had also given Emmett a rechargeable flashlight, a portable smoke detector and half a dozen other gadgets. Their adoptee had responded with what had become a common refrain for the evening. "Thank you, Nick. Now what the hell did you say this was?"

Emmett tore open another of Holly's packages. "A hat! A good, sensible hat to help me keep these addled brains together. Thanks. I don't need to ask any questions about this!" He blew her a kiss before he pulled the wool hat on his head with a laugh.

Holly sat back feeling a tug of satisfaction. She'd given Emmett handmade scarves, a thick, water-resistant hat, woolen socks, fleece-lined slippers, rainbow-colored candles, a sweater that matched the blue in his eyes and two plaid Pendleton blankets. The elderly man seemed genuinely overjoyed by each of her efforts.

But was that part of the holiday illusion? Wanting to preserve a childlike innocence, appearing to love every gift because it was the thought, not the price tag?

She looked at the presents still waiting under the tree. More of the Petrovich need for extravagance? Had he outshone her efforts without meaning to? Was it intentional, or was it simply some primitive male rite revolving around the need to buy gifts that required electricity or batteries?

The colored lights of the Christmas tree and warm glow of the fire softened her resentment. She'd expressed her views about gift giving to Nick often enough, but that didn't give her the right to dictate what he chose to bestow on their adoptee.

The sky-blue cardigan she'd given Emmett lay in a tousled heap on the compact disc player. Which was more valuable in the eyes of Emmett Snow? And did it matter anymore?

"This is the last gift from me." Nick started to hand Emmett a rectangular box, but in his eagerness, unwrapped it himself. "It's an electronic blood-sugar monitor. Now, before you shrink back in horror and hide your fingers, let me explain."

Holly watched and listened as Nick went through the process step by step, testing their adoptee's sugar level without the usual protest. She was impressed by Nick's thoughtfulness. The monitor was a gift that would improve the quality of Emmett's life more than anything else he'd received from either of them. When the electronic voice announced the test results, Emmett wanted a second go at it.

"There'll be time tomorrow." Nick pressed a hand to Emmett's knee. "We don't want you to get fanatical about it."

"Nick and I also have a mutual gift for you," Holly announced, getting up to turn off the compact disc player. She went to the hall closet and brought out the mandolin and *tamburitza*.

While Emmett relaxed in his wing chair, draped in scarves and wool blankets, Nick and Holly played *Narodi Nam Se Kralj Nebeski* together, followed by a series of traditional Christmas carols. Their voices rose in harmony, soon joined by Emmett's trembling tenor.

As they paused after a song, Emmett held up a hand, his expression quizzical. He stood and scurried to the window.

"You two better come over here." Emmett's voice reached Holly through the soft diffusion of holiday warmth. "Looks like we're in for some freezing rain."

Gradually Holly became aware of the sharp pings against the roof and windows, and she laid the mandolin on the love seat. Nick set his instrument down, then reached for her hand and helped her up. Together they joined Emmett at the picture window overlooking the sloping hill. The streetlight illuminated a sleeting shower of rain. In minutes the pellets of ice increased to a thundering bombardment of every surface of the house.

"Weather idiots on television. This wasn't in the fool forecast," Emmett muttered, pressing his face closer to the windowpane. "I'd say we'll be waking up to a good old-fashioned silver thaw."

"Maybe we'll have just the one shower." Holly didn't want to break the magical cocoon of euphoric joy they'd shared and she tried to add a note of optimism.

Nick checked the thermometer at the window's edge. "The mercury's dipped below twenty degrees. Whatever isn't ice could freeze on contact."

They shared a cup of hot tea and stood huddled near the window, watching the street turn to a shimmering river of ice.

"It's time I turned in. I'm not one for words—" Emmett began.

"Don't give us that!" Nick teased. "Every time you say you're not one for words, you start a ten-minute speech, you old ham!" Nick cuffed Emmett lightly on the chin. "Now what were you going to say?"

Emmett cuffed Nick back. "I wasn't going to make a speech. I just wanted to say I had a good time. In fact, it was great. And I wanted to ask if you two could spend the night?" The joviality was gone. There was a slight note of uncertainty in Emmett's tone. "I'm worried about the two of you gettin' home. The roads'll be dangerous. How about stayin' the night? I got sleepin' bags and extra robes. I got a sister who married money back East. She sends me a robe every Christmas. My closets are full of 'em."

"Emmett, we'll stay—" Holly began.

"Once I go to bed," he interrupted, "I'm dead to the world. I won't be getting up and botherin' you." He winked.

"No problem." Nick put his arm around Holly and drew her close. "Help us find those robes and sleeping bags, then you get to bed and bundle up. We'll open our gifts in private, Emmett, and we promise to keep the home fires burning."

Nick picked up a thin oblong box from under the tree. "For you, Holly."

With a timid smile she accepted the package. After unwrapping it with slow deliberate movements, she saw the logo of the jewelry store atop the box.

"Nick—" she began to protest.

"Go ahead. Open it."

She heard her own quick intake of air as a necklace slithered into her palm. The gold was cool against her skin, but an uncomfortable warmth gathered in her cheeks. The design was simple, elegant, perfect.

"Oh my God. It's beautiful, Nick," she stammered. "It's more than that, it's exquisite."

"Here, let me," he offered, fastening the clasp as she held her hair away from her nape. His fingers lingered on her neck, then slipped to her jawline. "The necklace is a reminder. We're both links in the Chain of Caring, and more importantly, Holly, this is a reminder of how much I care about you."

"I don't know what to say. Thank you." Her fingers moved to the base of her throat where the chain dipped into a V. She struggled to put her feelings more eloquently, but words escaped her.

Nick's fingers moved over Holly's shoulder and grazed the sensitive skin at the nape of her neck. She became intensely aware of the warmth of his touch and, at the same moment, the sound of the fire spitting and crackling as a log resettled against the grate.

The flame that had leaped into awareness soon after they met flared. While the sights and smells of Christmas surrounded her, she felt overwhelmed by the feel of Nick's thumb touching the clasp of her necklace, rolling the gold against her flesh in an erotic dance of promise.

Then with a clarity that surprised her, she felt like a traitor to her past and to the promises she'd made to herself. Each Christmas she'd allowed her parents' gifts to temporarily ease the empty ache within. Never again, she'd promised herself, would she fall so completely under the spell of the season.

The chain of gold around her throat was the pony and the clown and the hired Santa from her childhood. Holly swallowed hard as hot tears filled her eyes and slipped down her cheeks.

She turned away from Nick. Why was the past always waiting in the shadows, waiting to sabotage the joy of the present?

"You should save your tears for morning." Nick touched her chin and lifted her face to his gaze. "Croatians believe water is blessed by angels' wings on Christmas morning." He wiped the tears away and frowned when she tried to smother a sob. Fresh tears wet his fingertips. He bent low and kissed her cheek.

"Are these tears of joy, Holly?"

Holly closed her eyes against the pain, cursing herself for losing control. She wasn't being fair. Nick expressed his love in so many ways. Why not allow him this extravagance?

"Tears of joy, of course." She wiped her cheeks impatiently and knelt down beside the tree. "I hesitate to have you open this, Nick. I really didn't expect the necklace." Holly pulled a shoe-box-shaped package from under the tree.

The movement caused the royal-blue velvet robe she was wearing to open, giving Nick an alluring glimpse of a lacy bra and the rise of her breasts. Nick sat down and adjusted the folds of fabric in his lap.

"I knew I was taking a chance, giving you something so unusual." Holly moved into a sitting position and looked down at the gaily wrapped present. "But somehow I sensed you'd like it."

"Don't sound so apologetic. You know I'd treasure anything you gave me. Any clues? Animal, vegetable or mineral?" he asked as he tore off the paper.

"Try this. It's a vegetarian animal, and you'll probably think it's silly, but if you laugh, I'll turn it into a raging carnivore."

Nick opened the box and pushed the tissue aside. A wide-eyed sock monkey stared back at him with an ear-to-ear red cotton grin.

"Jocko." For a moment he wasn't certain he'd said the name aloud. Then he looked up at Holly. She'd heard him. There was a curious mixture of tenderness and surprise in her face. "Where did you find him?"

"What? Where did I find the monkey?" she asked quietly. "I made it. What did you call him?"

"Jocko." The tears that gathered in Nick's eyes seemed more a reflex than a conscious emotion. He cleared his throat forcefully and lifted the sock monkey from the crowded confines of the shoe box. "Ages ago my mother made a sock monkey for me for Christmas. I must have been about four or five. I remember being embarrassed because the other kids got toy trucks or guns and me, Nicholas Ivan Stjepan Petrovich—'' Nick set the stuffed animal on his knee and stared at the comic features ''—me, I got a homemade sock monkey with sad eyes and a goofy grin.''

''You were embarrassed, but you gave him a name?''

''Yeah, I loved the little guy. He was the only Croatian-speaking monkey in Chicago. We're not talking monkey chatter here. Jocko and I had a lot of deep conversations.''

Nick felt his throat grow tight again. He picked up one of the soft ribbed primate paws and rubbed it between his fingers, recalling the comfort that texture had brought thirty years ago.

''I guess you have to understand the way it was, Holly, so you can understand the way I am.'' His voice was thick, and the words felt heavy on his tongue. ''When I was a kid we didn't have Christmas trees. In fact, there were years when I was lucky to get a single gift. The traditions were intact—the sprouting of the wheat and the tricolor candle, water blessed by angels' wings, Christmas cakes brought by relatives, but as a child, I always wanted tangible proof of my parents' love. Sounds a little greedy, doesn't it?''

Nick looked into Holly's soft gray eyes. She was listening, letting him talk without airing her judgment of his meandering thoughts and boyhood foolishness, and he loved her for it. He loved her for the hours of affection, for every argument and opinion and endearment expressed. Her open features encouraged him to say more, to share the feelings he'd always held secret.

Is this when love grew stronger? he wondered for a fleeting second. Their lovemaking had been passionate, intense, satisfying, but it was after moments of emotional intimacy that he felt a quickening of attraction, a dull ache of need, the desire to be with this woman forever.

"I sometimes wonder," he mused, "if I'd been given all the toys I wanted, would I have studied architecture? It all comes together in the end, doesn't it, Holly? The pieces fall in place."

They were only inches apart, facing one another. Nick moved closer, adjusting the monkey on his knee. Their backs were against the love seat, their legs stretched out over the sleeping bags they'd zipped together to form one large bed.

"It comes together in the end, but the road is different, often bumpier, for some." She looked into the fireplace, her features contemplative. "You don't know how rich you were as a child, Nick, emotionally and spiritually. You were given a wealth of tradition, a sense of your people and their values."

"I didn't see it that way. As a kid, I would have preferred the trucks and the building set. Maybe that's why I feel the need to overdo now, to shower the people I care about with the tangible proof I never got."

"I'd call you a fool, Nick," Holly laughed and leaned against his shoulder, "but the way Emmett uses that word, I swear he's taken out the copyright. Don't you see? I was given a catalog and told to choose whatever gifts I wanted. You were given love, Nick."

"And the burden of not understanding what I was getting. I hated homemade gifts when I was four and five."

"So you kept your monkey a secret?"

Nick nodded and put his arm around her. "Yeah, ol' Jocko and I were buddies." He felt the tears gathering again and blinked them back. "Makes me feel bad now to think my mother never realized how much I secretly loved her gift. But why should that surprise me? This holiday season has been full of regrets and remembrances. On the other hand, it's been full of awakenings. I'm glad we met the way we did, under Emmett's roof. I don't know where I'd be tonight if it hadn't been for you."

"I would have been at home watching *It's A Wonderful Life* for the first time without my mother and crying into my popcorn because... well, because the reality of her death would hit me pretty hard. I thought of her tonight, Nick. I have my regrets and remembrances, too, but my life wouldn't have been this wonderful tonight without you."

She lifted her head from his shoulder and reached out to touch Jocko II. "I put some very special stuffing inside this guy," she whispered. "He's full of the hopes and dreams of a special little boy grown into manhood. He's stitched with love, Nick. My love."

She bit her lower lip as she realized what she'd said. Aloud.

"Holly. Do you realize how much I need you?" There was a tortured rasp in Nick's voice.

She turned her head at the sound, reacting in part to the sudden tensing along the sinewy muscles of his thigh where her forearm rested. Captured by the longing in his eyes, Holly sat up on her knees and put her arms around his neck.

Weaving his fingers through her thick auburn waves, Nick brought Holly's mouth down on his. His tongue flicked out to taste her, to trace the enticing curve of her lower lip, but his control ended there, at the corner of her mouth.

Nick held her face between his hands, his thumbs stroking the hollows beneath her cheekbones, as he studied her eyes, her half-parted lips.

"I feel a little crazy," he confessed. "I've been raised to believe this is the most joyous, wonderful night of the year, Holly. Tonight I feel a kind of rebirth—"

"Nick." She pressed a finger to his mouth.

"I love you." He spoke the words against her fingertips. "You must know that by now, but I want to say it aloud. Give it power. I want to make you understand how much and why and how often those words have passed through my mind for the past few weeks."

He kissed each eyelid, whispering her name as his lips moved back to her mouth. The kiss was ravaging, raw, a complete possession. His hands moved over the curve of her jaw, down the slender column of her neck, his fingertips catching briefly on the smooth chain of gold at the base of her throat.

He wanted to see her, all of her. His hands pressed against the cool satin collar of her robe for an instant, edging it back slowly to reveal the bra that caressed her breasts like a second skin. The velvet robe slipped to the edge of her shoulders, leaving a portion of her upper body open to his gaze.

Nick's focus moved to the teasing glimpse of lace at the rise of Holly's breasts. The warm orange glow of firelight mingled with the colored lights of the Christmas tree, heightening the mysteries hidden in shadow.

He rose up and took her in his arms, rolling her onto her back on the double cushion of sleeping bags and brushing his lips against the silken softness of her flesh, his tongue gliding down the valley between her breasts.

Holly felt as though she hovered between two planes—the reality of loving and the illusory world of being loved. Nick had said he loved her, but the words refused to penetrate. She allowed her mind to drift, concentrating only on the sensations that echoed the meaning of his words.

Everything that had pleased her in the past brought rapture tonight. She needed to catch her breath and sort things out, but there was no stopping, only colored lights and Nick's firelit features and his quick, uneven breathing.

What had Nick said earlier about water touched by angels' wings? The light, flickering caress of his tongue tormented her, sending frenzied ripples through her incoherent thoughts, until she lost control and his name was torn from her lips.

He moved up to capture the moans from her, to whisper endearments. As Nick took the lobe of her ear between his teeth, his fingertips touched the crest of each breast. She felt the texture of his long fingers through the sheer fabric of the lacy bra. Even in the dim light Holly sensed his hunger, and her own passion was doubled.

"We've memorized each other's bodies with our eyes. I want to learn you with my hands and mouth,

Nick.'' She flattened her palms against the black velvet lapels of his tartan robe, moving her thumbs out to stroke the smooth muscled flesh within her reach.

Making love with their robes on heightened the exhilaration of relearning the planes and hollows, the curves and textures of one another's bodies.

A gust of wind howled down the chimney, igniting the smoldering embers on the grate into blazing splendor. Holly felt the sudden flare of heat against the side of her face and the exposed line of her thigh. Her hands slipped beneath the sea of tartan plaid to find the smooth rounded curve of Nick's buttocks. Her fingertips trailed over his flesh, absorbing the shock of each of his measured thrusts. Her nails dug into his skin, the jolts of pleasure intensified, fanning the fire of their fused rhythm until the peak was within her reach. She closed her eyes against the explosion of sensations, holding fast to the image of angel wings fluttering, flying higher—to somewhere silver, flooded by the halo of a hundred shimmering moons.

As the flames in the fireplace became a sputtering, crackling presence, their passion flowed into contentment. Nick covered their bodies with the top layer of the two sleeping bags and kissed the damp curls beside Holly's ear.

"Do we need to turn the Christmas lights off?" She settled into the curve of his body.

"I put them on an automatic timer. They'll turn off in about—" Nick glanced at the clock on the mantel "—ten minutes."

"I was secretly hoping we could sleep bathed in that holiday glow. The colored bulbs give the room a touch of magic, an unreal light, like starlight."

"Haven't I given you magic enough, Holly?"

She moved against him with the feline indolence of a satisfied cat. "You don't come in five colors or twinkle, but you do give off a very masculine warmth. I should know. I'm still basking in it, Nick."

He chuckled into the blue velvet covering her shoulder. "How can I compete with a tree? Just wait. In ten minutes the tree will turn off, the room will grow dark—" his hand moved over the seductive curve of her hip "—and I'll be your starlight."

Eleven

If my mother could see me now, cooking the Christmas feast in the fireplace!" Nick loosened the scarf around his neck. He transferred the traditional *sarma*, stuffed cabbage, from the plate Holly held over to the pan on the makeshift grill. "In Chicago my Uncle Ivan would have smoked a small pig, and there'd be baskets of cakes." He turned to look at Holly. "I wish you could see it. The relatives, the noise, the Yule log and then there's the feasting, music, and dancing. All this chaos and confusion mixed with moments of solemnity."

"It's kind of hard to hold to tradition during an ice storm and power failure." She spoke in a good-natured tone as she set the plate on the hearth and reached for more kindling. "If confusion is a necessary part of a Croatian holiday, we're halfway to authentic now, and it isn't even noon."

Their banter was interrupted when Emmett tapped his finger against the barometer by the front picture window and clucked his tongue. He moved his attention to the thermometer. "We're down to ten degrees. Pretty low for these parts. Looks like the whole neighborhood's lost power. The radio says tree branches are bringin' most of the wires down. Phone's still workin', though. I'm goin' to start saving up scraps for the birds."

Nick frowned and stood up. Emmett had been nervous and slightly disoriented all morning. What if he'd been alone at a time like this?

If only Delilah Carpenter had agreed to a Christmas reunion. She'd contacted Nick three days earlier by registered mail, stating her interest in returning to Portland and seeing Emmett Snow, but expressing uncertainty about meeting him in the same paragraph.

Perhaps, Nick thought, if he could get their adoptee to focus on something for an extended period of time, it would take Emmett's mind off the storm, and the older man might relax and stop pacing.

"Emmett, why don't we listen to Christmas carols on your new compact disc player or look at one of the movies I rented?"

"Sure thing." The lines around Emmett's eyes crinkled. "I'll run out and hire a couple of squirrels to generate power. I appreciate the thought, but those things are useless when there ain't no electricity. We can't even light up the fool Christmas tree or use the microwave to cook our dinner. Excuse me. I'm goin' to call a coupla friends across town, wish them Merry Christmas and make sure they're doing all right."

"Friends?" Nick felt like a dolt with his monosyllabic reply.

"The guys I met on the stern-wheeler. Bernie and Gus and Ray. We've been keepin' in touch. Still planning that fishing trip on Mount Hood this spring." Picking up one of the blankets Holly had given him, Emmett draped it over his shoulders and brushed by Nick on his way to the kitchen.

Nick glanced over at Holly who sat cross-legged by the hearth. Her smile appeared a little too smug, too self-satisfied. "Emmett is wearing your sweater, your hat, your mittens and your homemade scarf, and now he's swathed in your blanket. Do I detect a bit of gloating?" He raised his eyebrows and moved toward her.

"Me? Gloat?" Holly stifled a laugh. "Surely you're not referring to the delicate balance involved in the art of gift giving?"

"Holly—"

"Because it doesn't apply. Emmett might be bundled up in the gifts that I gave him, but the electronic blood-sugar monitor is the one item under the tree that will benefit him the most in the long run. You put a lot of thought into choosing it, and you took the time to learn how to calibrate and use it. I'm not gloating. Here, help me move the coffee table over so I can set it."

"We're eating dinner in the living room?" Nick picked up the heavy table and helped her move it between the wing chairs and the love seat.

"The fireplace makes it the warmest room in the house." She wiped the surface with a cloth. "This will be the most unforgettable feast we'll ever have."

"Especially when I'm sitting here chewing on cabbage rolls and thinking about the fact that we made love on this very spot last night. How am I going to concentrate?"

"Concentrate? On a cabbage roll?"

"On our duet, on the ceremony of the wheat and candle, on anything?" Nick leaned across the coffee table until his lips hovered over hers. "You're turning our bed of roses into a buffet table."

"What can I say, Mr. Gourmand? *Bon appétit!*" Holly dropped the dust cloth. "What makes you think you'll be the only one having trouble with concentration?"

Nick placed the tricolor candle in a small glass filled with corn and garlic cloves, then set the glass in the center of the bowl of wheat. The wheat had been cut to an even length as dictated by tradition.

"I'm gettin' hungry," Emmett grumbled from his position in the wing chair. "Don't tell me you gotta harvest that wheat with some miniature thresher before we eat our Christmas dinner, or I just might lose my patience."

"What patience?" Nick chuckled, then lit a match and held it over the candle.

The meal went smoothly from cabbage rolls with a slight barbecued flavor to tossed green salad.

"Should we break the *Pogača* and find out who's going to be rich this year?"

"The what?" Emmett leaned forward.

"The sweet bread I had baked with the quarter in it." Nick passed it to Holly, who broke off a piece, and then gave the loaf to Emmett.

"Makes a lot of sense." Emmett laughed and broke off a large piece. "Paying the deli baker five dollars so you have something to put a quarter in. Tradition, bah. Whoever finds the two bits gets rich, huh?"

"Right." Nick completed the circle, breaking off his portion. The next few minutes were absorbed in the search for the quarter.

"Save the crumbs for the birds," Emmett warned. He left his segment of sweet bread on his napkin. "Well, I didn't get the quarter, but I'm rich in other ways." He looked from Nick to Holly. "Thank you for stayin' the night. I was nervous at the thought of you two driving home and maybe the thought of being alone. I'm not one for words—" Emmett glanced at Nick and laughed. "I've got to stop saying that. I'm gettin' better at expressing myself. Right now I only need two words. Thank you."

"*Adeste Fideles*," Holly began singing softly into the wool of her muffler as she plodded through ice-encrusted snow to the woodshed. She stopped singing, choosing instead to listen to the eerie sounds of power lines creaking and tree limbs cracking beneath the weight of more than an inch of ice.

She would have been satisfied with a white Christmas. Three or four inches of pristine snow. The silver thaw had frozen the city. Residents of the West Hills and scattered areas of Portland were without power. Travelers were stranded, families separated, lives endangered.

Nick had volunteered to knock on the doors of all the neighboring houses to see if anyone needed help. Emmett was busy making phone calls to his friends.

So far, Gus, Bernie and Ray were with family or being looked after by thoughtful neighbors.

Holly was left to tend the fire. With the house growing colder by the hour, she'd decided it was time to gather another load of wood.

And think.

What was she going to do about Nick Petrovich? How did he fit into her life? The old-world charm was in full bloom. Though he joked about some of the Croatian customs, he observed the ceremonies with reverence. She'd looked up several times during the Christmas meal to find him staring at the candle nestled in the bowl of wheat with a faraway look in his eyes. His expression grew serious as he snuffed out the flame with a piece of *Pogača* dipped in wine.

It was at that moment, as the smoke wafted upward, obscuring her view of him, Holly realized she would have to reexamine her reasons for loving Nick. To accomplish that, it might be necessary to cut back on their time together.

"Holly?"

She turned at the sound of his voice. Nick was standing in the snow just beyond the woodshed, hands in his jacket pockets, his expression unreadable.

"I decided to gather more wood for the fireplace," she said hesitantly, nodding toward the woodpile. She'd been looking forward to a little solitude, time to organize her thoughts and sort out her warring emotions. "How are all the neighbors doing?"

"There's a tree limb down on one roof and another house has frozen pipes that burst overnight." Nick moved to her side and began helping her load wood into the carrier. "They've got plenty of food and firewood. Everyone's watching out for each other. It's nice to see people pulling together."

"Especially on Christmas," she added.

"Holly." Nick put his hand on the wedge of wood she was about to pick up. "I need to talk to you."

"What's wrong?"

"Nothing is wrong." His fingers moved down the bark until they met her hand. "In fact, things have never been so right."

"Right?" She allowed herself a light laugh as he took her gloved hand in his. "We're icebound, Nick, without heat or lights. The pipes could freeze, tree limbs and telephone poles might crush the house—"

His features softened. "You forgot lions, tigers and bears. Wild animals might eat all our food."

"I'm serious. We could be stranded here for a week."

"Sounds wonderful. A week together."

"Nick." She pried her hand loose and tried to lift the piece of firewood, but he held it firmly atop the stack. "Did the neighbors share a little Christmas wine with you? Why are you in this lighthearted mood?"

"Because of you." Gently he urged her away from the woodpile. "I want to thank you for making this a perfect celebration."

"We were both a part of that, Nick."

"Maybe. I just want you to know I'm thankful. I feel fulfilled, and I don't want the feeling to end." He reached inside his jacket pocket and pulled out a small gift-wrapped box. With quick deft movements he tore the paper off and held the box in his palm.

"When I bought this, it was meant to be a friendship ring of sorts." He opened the box and removed a gold ring. In the bright light reflected from the snow, Holly could see the glitter of diamonds.

"It was an impulsive gesture, but by now you know I give in to my impulses." With one hand he touched the wool cap on her head, then moved his fingers down to caress the waves that framed her face. "I'm glad I did, because I'm asking you to marry me, Holly. I never want this feeling of fulfillment to end."

Long seconds passed before she found her voice.

"I'm sorry. Nick, I want to say yes..."

"You just did."

"No, no, that wasn't yes."

"I love you. I'm sure of that. For the first time in my life I want to make a commitment."

"Nick, you can't be sure of anything. It's the season. For the past six weeks we've been living in another time zone. The delusional zone. Holiday time. We can't trust our feelings. We haven't spent enough time away from Emmett's home to know for sure."

"Know what, Holly?"

"This is Christmas. We're in a cloud, and I learned early in life not to trust this time of year. You know that."

She stepped back and lowered her head. "My parents bought my trust every year, like they were paying a premium on some kind of insurance policy. For years they made me believe the magic, and then there was always the letdown."

"That was a long time ago, Holly. Things change." He stepped closer, wedging her between his chest and the stack of wood. She was forced to face him.

"I'm worried that I've been using you, both you and Emmett, to fill this void in my life." She rested her palms against the front of his jacket. "I've been trying to have the ideal Christmas as long as I can remember—''

"Wasn't it ideal?" Nick was smiling, an odd, gentle expression that tugged at her heart.

"Of course, it was wonderful, Nick. I might go on thinking that for a few days or a week, but then something will cave in, and I'll be faced with this painful reality."

"What reality?"

"The truth is Christmas forces us to be perfect people for a day and to create expectations we feel obliged to fulfill."

"Is that so wrong?"

"Yes!" Her tone was more emphatic than she intended. "We're forced to confront who we are and what we want, where we're going."

"Where are we going, Holly?"

"Don't, please. Now you're forcing me to think about the issue of marriage. I can't, Nick. Let me enjoy the rest of this day. For once in my life maybe all the wonderful feelings will last."

"They will." He touched her cheek. "Trust me. In the meantime, Holly, would you accept this as a ring of friendship?"

She looked down at the slim golden band, seeing the details of the wheat pattern for the first time. "The wheat like in the Croatian ceremony, the ties to your roots. I'll wear it, Nick, in friendship."

She took off her glove and watched with misted eyes as he slipped it onto her finger. "Do you realize this is where we met?" she asked softly. "Right here by the woodshed? Did you propose marriage to me here intentionally?"

"No." Nick pulled her into his arms. "Impulse again." He sighed. "I was hoping you'd say yes, Holly, to make my Christmas complete."

"I didn't say yes or no, Nick. I love you. I want you to understand it's not you I distrust. It's the season."

"Emmett, you feeling all right?" Nick stepped into the older man's bedroom. Emmett sat on the edge of his four-poster bed, holding the gold star Nick had given him at arm's length and twirling it when it lost momentum.

"I'm fine," Emmett said with a sigh.

"Feeling a little down?" Nick sat in the rocking chair opposite Emmett. "The ice is melting. According to the radio, the roads should be clear by tomorrow."

"Yep." Emmett nodded, staring intently at the hologram within the star. "We got lights and hot meals and a warm house. I've appreciated your being here. Been three whole days. You and Holly can get back to your lives. Your *separate lives*."

"Our separate lives? Emmett, what's bothering you? A little holiday letdown? Maybe we can go sledding. It might be a little slushy for it, but—"

"She turned down your marriage proposal. I was feedin' the birds out back. I heard." Emmett stopped spinning the star and looked up at Nick. "I'm not one to butt into other people's personal business, but you two are different. You're special to me, and I'd like to see the two of you settle down for life, so you won't be lonely when you're older."

Emmett stood up. He handed the star to Nick, then walked to the bedroom window.

"The issue isn't closed exactly," Nick tried to assure the older man. He looked down at the hologram, the tiny earth within the star's confines. "She didn't say no, Emmett. We're going to wait a little while, give it some time."

"Give it some time? Don't be foolish, Nick. Listen to an expert, someone who learned firsthand about time. When Delilah and I were young, we had a favorite love song, *our* song. It was called 'When I Grow Too Old to Dream.' Back then I never imagined the day would come when I'd have white hair. I guarantee you this, Nick, dreams don't die, but they can fade with time."

"Holly and I will continue to see each other—"

"But this could go on for weeks, months, a year. Maybe you two need some incentive."

"What do you mean? Incentive?"

"A symbol of hope that your love will prevail." Emmett stood erect, his shoulders thrust back. "I've got it. I'm not takin' my Christmas tree down till you two agree to get married."

"But, Emmett." Nick choked back a laugh. "Holly will just have to make a decision when she's ready."

"I'm not trying to force the issue, but the tree will stand—" Emmett held up a finger "—as a not-so-gentle reminder from someone who knows."

Twelve

I'll miss coming here every two weeks." Roxanne Shelton took a pair of dark glasses out of the breast pocket of her jacket.

"Judging from the way you've always grimaced, I never imagined you actually enjoyed the wax removal. Just a minute, let me have a closer look." Holly tilted the light down and rechecked the puffiness on Roxie's upper lip. "Still a tiny bit red in this area. Let me put a little more powder on the right side."

"It's you, Holly. We both know I needed the wax treatments, but that's for the outer person. You've helped the inner me by being my friend, my confidante, my therapist. You talked me into applying for the anchor position and taking chances. Like the electrolysis."

"You would have chosen it eventually. I'm just happy you're having it done in Los Angeles, Roxie. There are certain advantages to anonymous living. No one will recognize you."

"That's what I mean. You always have the right answers. Are you sure you and Sara won't move to Seattle and act as consultants for my talk show? *My own talk show.* I still can't believe it."

"I do. You're perfect for the job."

"Will you consider my idea?"

"What idea?"

"The one involving you and Sara? You can move to Seattle, open your salon up there instead of in Portland, act as consultant to the show—"

"Whoa!" Holly turned off the overhead light. "How about a compromise? Sara and I could appear on your program every few months and do a total make-over?" She hopped onto the counter and leaned against the mirror. "We could fly up, pick a member of the audience on day one, start the make-over and work with a professional clothes buyer, then return to the show on day two with the results."

"Great idea. You talk to Sara, and I'll talk to my producer. Are you coming to the station's farewell party?"

"Sorry." Holly shook her head. "Nick made reservations for a bed-and-breakfast place at the coast."

"In mid-January?"

"He thinks the Oregon coast is romantic year round. But then he feels the same way about the mountains. We spent a few nights at Timberline Lodge and went skiing—"

"But I thought you wanted time away from Nick so you could think about your big decision."

"We're spending time apart, but I'm discovering that I think about the decision more often when I'm with Nick." Holly looked down at the friendship ring on her finger.

"Mind telling me where your thoughts are leading you?" Roxie put on her sunglasses and slipped a scarf over her hair.

"I wish I knew. I'm waiting for the magic to fade. The fog will clear, and my prince might turn into a frog."

"I've seen Nick. If the frog has a brother who lives in Seattle, lead me to his pond!"

Nick held the registered letter in his hand. For two days he'd been struggling with complicated legal and business details regarding the merger that would open up his design programs for international distribution. So he welcomed this interruption, especially when he recognized the return address.

Dear Mr. Petrovich,
Thank you for being so understanding on the phone when I spoke to you in December. I want you to know I'm getting closer to making a decision about journeying to Portland to visit Emmett Snow.

Ever since the investigator contacted me, Emmett's been on my mind. We had such wonderful times together that I sometimes wonder if my imagination has embellished the past. I could live with the memories of the special friendship we had, but I keep thinking about the time we could share together creating new memories.

Mr. Petrovich, if you could write and describe the type of reception I might expect from Emmett, it would help in my decision.

There's another matter I hope you can help me with. You've mentioned Holly Peterson, your fellow volunteer who does total make-overs. If I decide to visit Portland to see Emmett, I would be in need of her services. Thank you very much.

Sincerely,
Delilah Carpenter

Nick reread the letter. How could he anticipate Emmett's reaction to the sight of Delilah on his doorstep? Forty years had passed. There might be misunderstandings on both sides. There might be old doubts....

"It's not you I distrust. It's the season."

There was nothing predictable about Holly Peterson's response to the question he'd asked on Christmas day. Her request for more time had mystified him at first. She had feared the warmth and magic of the holidays would end. Four weeks had passed, and the illusion, as Holly had called it, showed no signs of dissipating.

Nick looked down at the letter in his hand. No, it was different for Emmett and Delilah. Emmett had chosen his career and family responsibility. He had loved and lost. There was no similarity.

Who could define the reasons people loved? Love was unique to each individual, to each couple. Losing was equally diverse and always painful, and Nick couldn't bear to entertain the idea of losing Holly.

He opened a desk drawer and took out pen and paper. Would Emmett and Delilah be happier with their memories? What had he done? Was he setting them up for another loss? He leaned over the kitchen counter and began to write.

Dear Delilah,

I just received your letter and debated for a short time about how to respond. I'll be honest with you. I can't predict how Emmett Snow will react to seeing you after forty years. I think it's best that I describe Emmett as I see him.

He's isolated himself during the past ten years, since selling out his interest in the company that bought Snow's Shoes. Recently he began breaking out of that shell of isolation and is becoming more involved with the outside world. He's finding the strength he thought was diminishing.

He's stubborn, opinionated, determined and deeply sentimental. I think he's what would be considered a dashing figure of a man, still tall and lean, with an eye for the classic cut in clothing. His hair is thinning slightly at the temples, and time has turned it white.

He has a list of things he wants to do this year. Perhaps you will be able to accomplish a few of those things together. I'm not afraid to admit that Emmett has tried my patience at times, and that of my fellow volunteer, Holly Peterson, but we love him dearly.

In the past two months he's collected all of the movies in which you had roles and plays them frequently on his VCR. I believe you're on his mind, Delilah, and still in his heart.

Should you decide to visit Portland, I'll be happy to arrange your lodging. I'll be anxious to help you make arrangements for a day at Holly's salon, but please allow me to cover the cost for a day of pampering, my treat, before you meet Mr. Snow. I hope you won't be able to turn down my offer for a total make-over...

Feeling like a conspirator, Nick finished the letter, suggesting they keep the plan a secret. As he addressed the envelope, he couldn't help wondering how Holly would react when she discovered the woman in her salon chair was Delilah Carpenter.

"Nice and cloudless. We'll get a good look at the volcano in this weather." Emmett leaned against the porch railing of his home and studied the blue February sky.

Holly stood in the doorway watching the figures of Emmett and Nick with the city of Portland as a backdrop. She inhaled deeply, satisfied with the weather and her adoptee's mood. She and Nick were taking a day trip with Emmett to see the Mount Saint Helens' visitors' center north of Portland.

"Could we sit down for a minute before we leave?" Emmett asked, heading back into the house.

"Sure, we're a little early, and it looks like you're well prepared for the trip," Holly assured him.

"I've got news," Emmett announced to Nick and Holly. "Good news." He walked into the living room and sat down in his wing chair beside the fireplace.

"Well?" Holly settled on the love seat beside Nick. She leaned closer.

"My friend Gus drove me to the clinic yesterday, and I saw my doctor." Emmett spoke slowly like a storyteller relishing his tale. He looked from Nick to

Holly. "I can stop taking the oral medication. They think I'll be able to control my diabetes with diet and exercise."

"That's terrific." Knowing what this meant to Emmett, Holly felt tears gather in her eyes. She stood up and hugged him while Nick offered his hand.

"Yessir." Emmett beamed with pride. "The doctor says the monitor and the exercise bike helped a lot, and he says the diet Holly forced me to stick to was just as important. You two are a damn good team."

Holly frowned, wanting to change the subject back to Emmett's health. For the past six weeks every conversation at Emmett's home had included a few random remarks about teamwork, companionship, the joy of marriage, the challenges of parenting, the importance of heritage—all this from a seventy-two-year-old bachelor.

Holly didn't know what was worse: Emmett's persistent remarks or the presence of the withering Christmas tree. Nick had disconnected the lights long ago and moved the tree far away from the fireplace. All of the heirloom ornaments had been removed.

As the weeks passed and branches drooped, a few of the silver balls had shattered on the hardwood floor. Tiny spiders emerged, spinning webs from the tinsel star atop the tree to the curtain, decorating the fading tree with little threads that caught the sunlight, marking the passage of time. The tree had become a fourth party in the room, a presence, a reminder of Emmett's outrageous vow.

What a paradox, Holly thought. As the tree grew weaker, her faith in the love she felt for Nick Petrovich grew stronger.

It was only a lingering doubt, a niggling distrust that kept her from giving Nick a final answer. Surprisingly, part of that distrust was centered here, in Emmett's home.

Their commitment to him would end in less than three weeks, and they'd met and fallen in love in these rooms. Even though they'd begun spending more time away from the house, taking two and three-day trips outside of Portland, it was here that her love for Nick burned brightest, where the memories of her most precious Christmas enveloped her and here where she realized the magic was lasting.

When their commitment to Emmett was over, and their visits to his home ceased, would that love burn as brightly in Nick's condo or in her Victorian?

"It's going to be a long day." Nick curled his fingers through hers. "We'd better get a good start so we can catch a peek at the volcano while the sky is clear."

She squeezed Nick's hand and stood up. As she moved toward the entryway, sunlight dappled the withering boughs of the tree. Her eyes followed the silvery spiderwebs to the star of tinsel. Its silver surface shimmered with a luminous white glow. She stared at it for brief seconds before moving to Emmett's side.

"Pretty, huh? You know, I swear that star gets brighter every day." Emmett gave her a knowing little smile. "The fool tree might die on me and turn to dust, but not the star, Holly. Some things seem to have a second life."

Thirteen

My goodness, you're going for the total treatment, Lily." Holly glanced down at her client's schedule card.

"Massage, manicure, pedicure, facial, hair color and styling, makeup consultation and wardrobe." The white-haired woman sitting in the salon chair counted off the appointments on her fingers as she listed them. "I intend to end this day feeling totally renewed, but don't get me wrong. I'm also a realist."

"What do you mean?"

"I've always believed changes have to come from within, and I've worked on that." The older woman stared intently at Holly's reflection in the mirror. "Has anyone done a psychological follow-up on people who have one of these total overhauls? It would be fascinating to know how long the miracle lasts for each of them."

"I think that depends on how unhappy the clients are with different aspects of their lives," Holly commented with a shrug. "I've given it a lot of thought. I'm a little surprised. You're the first customer who's brought up the subject. Are you a psychologist?"

"Heavens, no!" Lily laughed. "If I were, I probably wouldn't be sitting here telling you I don't believe in those miracles when down deep, I want one. I want you to take forty years off of the sixty-five I've lived."

"Sixty-five? You look far younger. You're very attractive, Lily. Everyone needs to be pampered now and then, but you hardly need lessons on how to enhance your hair and face. There must be a special occasion coming up."

"I'm not at liberty to discuss my personal life." Lily looked down at her hands. "You see, I have a benefactor. He insisted on treating me to this day of pampering, and one of the conditions is that I not discuss the particulars with anyone. Especially the stylists here at the salon."

"You realize you're bound to make everyone twice as curious, don't you?"

"Of course. But isn't that the fun of it? We'll just have to concentrate on you, Holly. Now go ahead and put the makeup on. Teach me a few new tricks. I used to be a makeup artist years ago when the situation called for it."

"What situation?"

"Sorry. No questions. I forgot. Perhaps it's best if I don't tease you with any personal remarks." Lily closed her eyes and took a deep breath while Holly began applying foundation. After an awkward silence they began talking about makeup.

A mysterious benefactor? Holly's imagination worked overtime. On the average, she knew her clients' life story and at least one deep secret by the end of a full session. Lily fascinated her. There was a familiar cadence to her voice and a practiced air, a control she maintained over her features.

While Holly worked to add contour to Lily's cheeks, enlarge her eyes and reshape her brows, her client turned the tables and began delving into Holly's personal life.

"What a lovely wedding ring." Lily touched Holly's wrist and studied the ring. "How long have you been married?"

"I'm not. It's actually a friendship ring, of sorts."

"I was going to say you have a generous friend, of sorts. Is the relationship serious?"

"Yes, but I'm waiting to be sure. And you're right. He is generous, if not extravagant at times. I still have a little trouble with that." Holly found herself telling Lily about the volunteer work she did with Nick, about Emmett Snow and the wonderful Christmas they'd shared.

Holly rarely spoke of her own life with clients. She focused on their lives because it allowed her a glimpse into their expectations. Professional and managerial women often visited the salon every six months for a routine consultation. They wanted their hair and makeup to reflect their position, and usually they wanted a minimum of fuss. Job applicants, candidates for career advancement, brides—these were people with a specific purpose. She had a special love for the clients who were the recipients of gift certificates, those in search of some fun and those who needed a psychological lift.

Lily was a fascinating combination of all of those types. Her air of mystery challenged Holly, whose nature it was to draw people out, to ask the appropriate questions and to act as a sounding board.

Lily seemed to be ruminating on Holly's last comment. "So you're afraid when your commitment to this Mr. Snow is over, you'll lose that sense of home and belonging you feel whenever you're in his house? And on top of that, you're saying you don't trust Christmas?"

"Everything sounds so simple when you say it. Of course, my fears are more complicated than that, Lily. I have to laugh. When my clients have problems, the answers are clear. When it comes to this dilemma with Nick, all I can do is wait until some inner voice tells me everything will work out."

"I wish I were a ventriloquist right now."

"Why?"

"I could pretend to be that inner voice and speed things up." Lily shook her head. "I'm not making fun of you. I think the answers always come from within. Sometimes it takes a while for them to get to the surface. Sometimes it takes a lifetime, and then it's too late. Or almost too late."

"I'm only thirty-two."

"But while you wait for that inner voice, which could end up being nothing more than a faint whisper lost in the hum of the air conditioner, someone else might come along and catch your eye and start you wondering about a whole new set of problems."

"You sound experienced, Lily."

"Water under the bridge." The woman in the chair sighed and brushed the comment away with her hand. "Speaking of liquids, I would love another glass of that wonderful Chablis."

The make-over was completed. After Lily praised the staff effusively, she turned to Holly. "Time for our shopping trip."

"Oh, I'm not the clothing consultant. That's Phyllis—"

"But I want you to come with me."

Holly was flustered. "I'll have to talk to Phyllis."

"She left early," Sara explained from the end of the counter. "Family emergency of some sort."

Lily shrugged innocently, slipped a sizable tip under the hand mirror at Holly's station and closed her purse. "I'll be waiting by the front desk." She paused, looked at herself in the mirror and straightened her shoulders. "Maybe it isn't a miracle, but it sure feels like one."

A short time later Holly put on her coat and approached Lily. "I think I should emphasize again that I'm not a professional wardrobe consultant."

"Oh, that's fine. The important thing is that I like you. Judging from your appearance you have good taste. Let's start shopping. Now I'm a size ten, and I hate drab colors, but I'm not fond of anything shockingly bright."

Holly glanced down at the amount listed on Lily’s schedule card. ‘‘You could buy every color of the rainbow and a nun’s habit with this allowance.’’

‘‘Ignore it. I have no intention of taking advantage of my generous benefactor. I need five things, Holly. A good coat for this Portland weather, a sweater, wool slacks, a dress that fits the miracle your salon just performed and lingerie. Lots and lots of beautiful lingerie.’’

‘‘You’re early,’’ Nick whispered into Holly’s ear as he welcomed her at the door.

‘‘Traffic was light, the elevator was empty...’’ She paused when he leaned against the wall and stroked her back. ‘‘And I’m always anxious to see you, Nick. What time are we supposed to go over to Emmett’s?’’

‘‘Six-thirty.’’

‘‘He’s so excited about your surprise. Imagine discovering one of Delilah’s films on tape. Emmett thought he’d seen them all.’’

‘‘I have the scene cued up if you’d like a sneak preview. Come into the living room and sit down. It’ll just take a minute.’’

Holly slipped out of her coat and settled on the sofa. Though she rarely talked about her work, she was anxious to tell Nick about the mysterious client she’d devoted most of her day to. It could wait for the ride to Emmett’s house. Nick dimmed the lights and sat down beside her holding the remote control.

‘‘You’ll love this. It’s one of those great entrance scenes that Delilah does so well,’’ he promised. Nick lifted the remote unit and, instead of pointing it at the VCR, he aimed it toward the far end of the living room. A woman stepped through the kitchen entrance into the dim light of the larger room.

"Lily!" Holly choked the name out. "What are you doing here?" With sudden clarity the pieces fell into place. "Oh, my God. Are you Emmett's Delilah?"

"Now, now, darling. Treat me like a professional, and let me complete my entrance scene. I'm rather proud of what we accomplished today," Delilah said with a laugh. She moved toward the sofa and turned slowly before bending down to kiss both Holly and Nick on the cheek.

"Beautiful." Nick applauded softly.

"I can't believe it." Holly placed her hand between Nick's palms. "You orchestrated all of this without telling me?"

"I assumed you'd feel it was too extravagant a gesture." Nick stood and gently pulled Holly to her feet. "And I didn't want to get your hopes up if things didn't work out."

"But they did." Lily hugged Holly. "Let's hurry. I'm saving my grand entrance for Emmett."

"Of course," Holly mumbled a numb response. Her thoughts were scattered, panicked. She'd spent the day baring her soul to Delilah, even revealing her feelings about Nick and the marriage proposal.

Holly watched as Nick helped Delilah put on her new winter coat. The two seemed to have a warm rapport. What would prevent Delilah from telling Nick about Holly's innermost thoughts?

Please, not yet, Holly thought. *It isn't time.* She wanted to enjoy the reunion of two old friends this evening. The last thing she needed was a confrontation with whatever the future held for her and Nick.

* * *

"Well, cue the fool tape up so I can get a look at Delilah. What year did you say this movie was released? Where's it been all this time?" Emmett took the video cassette from Nick. "What's the title?" He raised the cardboard box higher. "The R-reunion of Em-mett and Delilah? Nick, what the hell—"

Nick opened the front door with a flourish. Delilah stood on the threshold, tears glistening in her eyes.

"Emmett!" She raised a hand to her mouth and smothered the small cry that followed. Nick touched her elbow and helped her into the living room.

Emmett dropped the cassette on the floor. Slowly he raised his hand to his chest and took a step toward them. "I don't believe my eyes. It's you, it's really you, Delilah?"

"In the flesh," Nick answered, brushing by the dying Christmas tree as he moved to draw the old friends closer together. "This is a belated Christmas surprise, Emmett."

Delilah and Emmett embraced awkwardly at first, then in a fierce caress. They became completely absorbed with one another, and Nick turned, looking at the lone figure in the entryway. Tears streaked Holly's cheeks. He took her in his arms, massaging her back in wide comforting circles.

"You'll forgive me the extravagance, won't you?"

"Of course, you can't put a price tag on love or friendship. They're both priceless gifts. Emmett and Delilah may not choose to share their lives, but you've given them a chance to find that out. It's the most unselfish, wonderful thing you've ever done."

Weaving her fingers through his hair, she drew his lips down on hers. The kiss was gentle, a whisper against his mouth. Nick closed his eyes and enjoyed the feel of Holly's body against his own. Glancing into the living room was a bit like staring at a reflection in a mirror—a man and woman embracing, talking softly.

"Perhaps you two need some time alone," Nick suggested. "Holly and I will start some coffee."

"Thank you, Nick." Emmett's hoarse murmur sounded faraway.

"Emmett's raising his voice," Holly noted from her perch on the kitchen counter. She took another bite of apple from the fruit and cheese platter they'd prepared.

"So I hear. Delilah's isn't exactly whispering, either." Nick topped a wafer-thin cracker with a slice of Brie.

"Do you think we should bring the coffee and the food out now or give them more time?"

"I don't want to interfere." Nick popped a grape into his mouth and glanced at the kitchen doorway. "After forty years they probably have a lot to discuss."

The voices from the living room grew louder. Nick paced the kitchen floor, studying the tiles intently. "Sounds like Emmett blames Delilah for not letting him know how badly she wanted her own career."

Holly nodded. "Now she's denying it. She thinks he was too devoted to the family business—" Holly nibbled on a piece of kiwi fruit "—and he wasn't impulsive or passionate enough to pursue her."

Nick chewed on a slice of dried apricot. "They both sound pretty upset. He seems to think she was sheltered by marriage and kids—"

"While he ended up alone and lonely." Holly bit into a piece of Swiss cheese and contemplated the holes in the remainder of the slice.

There was another interlude of quiet as both listened to the conversation.

"Why do you think we feel compelled to do this play-by-play instant replay?" Nick leaned against the opposite counter, looking up at the kitchen ceiling.

"We probably want to tie their problems up in a neat easy-to-solve package."

"Maybe. Come on, Emmett," Nick said under his breath. "Don't be so stubborn. Can't you put the past behind you?"

"I feel like I did when I was a kid, listening to my parents fight. Wondering how it would end. Do Croatians argue?"

Nick lowered his head and stared at Holly in surprise. The corners of his mouth twitched slightly. "Are you serious? Haven't I shown my capacity in that area? I know I'm even tempered, but we've had our moments—"

"I mean your parents. Did they lock horns now and then?"

"Sure." Nick finished the last of the cheese. "They argued about money, because there was never enough in those days. And they argued about me, whether I should get my own *tamburitza* or borrow my father's. You know, normal, run-of-the-mill arguments."

Emmett and Delilah's voices competed for dominance in the next room. Nick turned to face the doorway, then looked back at Holly.

"Now you and me, we'd never argue about money or careers or parenting. Never." He approached the counter where she sat. "Because we love each other too much, and we both know it's not worth the heartache. And we'd hardly have any reason to argue about whether or not our child gets their own personal *tamburitza*—"

"Mandolin," Holly corrected.

"Hmm, the poor child can play both. Or we'll have two kids. It'll be like that scene of dueling banjos." Nick stepped up to the kitchen counter, placing a palm on either side of her legs, and then leaned forward until his face was inches from hers. His eyes were warm and searching, his expression expectant.

Holly looked down to avoid staring into his intense gaze. He was wearing a plaid shirt and gray suspenders. There was no escape from his old-world charm.

"We shouldn't be having this discussion, Nick. It's silly."

"We're having this discussion," Nick spoke from between clenched teeth, "because we're both upset that Delilah and Emmett are out in the living room fighting and we're both afraid she might walk out of here and back to California and leave him alone. We love him, and we don't want to see him hurt."

"Then maybe we should take the damn fruit and cheese platter to the living room and force them to calm down!"

"Nice idea, Holly." Nick backed away, hands on his hips. "But we ate the bleeping fruit and cheese platter, and all we can offer is coffee and four grapes."

"Fine! That's one grape for each of us and a gallon of coffee!"

Nick held up his palms. "Let's calm down. Both of us. First tell me why you're so upset?"

"Because I don't want you shoving talk of two kids with dueling banjos down my throat. I'm not ready to make a decision, Nick!"

"I know. You're waiting until our commitment to Emmett ends. You're afraid your perfect Christmas was an illusion that won't last, so you're waiting until God knows when to find out whether it's lasted."

"You talked to Delilah?"

"Hell, no. I've talked to *you*, Holly. I know every excuse by heart! I've been patient, and I'll continue to be patient, but dammit, Holly, it can't be Christmas forever."

"Oh, dear." A female voice came from the doorway. "Perhaps you two need to be alone."

Holly and Nick turned. Delilah and Emmett were standing in the kitchen doorway, their eyes full of concern.

"Why don't the both of you head on home now?" Emmett stepped forward. "Delilah and I are having a great time catchin' up on things. I can call a cab to take her back to her hotel. Don't you worry. No need for the two of you to wait on us. We could be up all night. It's a wonderful thing you've done, giving us this chance to renew our friendship."

"There's coffee ready if you care for some," Nick said, quietly reaching out to shake Emmett's hand.

"You two take some time out for the happy memories, okay?"

"You're giving *us* advice?" Emmett took a cup off the tray and offered Delilah coffee. "We're just rehashing old history now. We'll work our way up to pleasantries later."

The tension between Holly and Nick eased slightly when they joined the other couple in laughter. They said their goodbyes in the kitchen. On the way through the living room Holly couldn't help looking at the drooping boughs of the dying tree.

She recalled the day they'd spent in the Oregon countryside in early December. The tree had been a symbol of new beginnings for them. Had it become a symbol of her undying love for Nick, or would her love die with the tree?

Nick waited for her in the entryway. He smiled at her, that wonderful, gentle, mystical smile she'd grown to feel was kept only for her.

"We just had a very stupid argument." She took a deep breath and exhaled. "We *argued* about *arguments*. Delilah must think we have the brains of sewer mice."

"Sewer mice? Don't you mean—"

"I don't want to discuss it." Holly's tone was emphatic. "Nick, I think it might be a good idea if we spend some time apart."

"Not see each other at all?"

"I'm not sure. Our agreement with Emmett is almost over. I think we should share time together here, but—"

"But you don't want to share a bed with me until you have things straightened out in your mind?"

"I know it sounds cold and calculating, but I need to distance myself, get my thoughts straight."

"And what about me? I told you in the kitchen I've been more than patient. Now I'm supposed to be a saint? There's a limit, Holly."

"Are you forgetting that I'm proposing equally saintlike behavior for myself? I'd rather spend my nights with you, Nick, but it's too painful now. I need time."

"And I need you, Holly." Nick put his hand on the doorknob. "What's it going to be?"

"We'll have to take that decision one day at a time."

Fourteen

Nick maneuvered his Mercedes around one of West Hills' winding curves. Emmett had called that morning, asking him to drop by the house. Would Holly be there? The question returned as he nosed the car around the final turn.

Seven days ago, just half a week after the reunion with Delilah, Emmett had formally asked both Nick and Holly to suspend their visits. Their adoptee said he needed time to rekindle his friendship with Delilah in private.

It had been more than ten days since Nick had seen Holly, ten days since they'd had that ridiculous argument in Emmett's kitchen. He'd been tempted to send jewelry, flowers, balloons, candy—even a singing clown, but none of those gifts could say what was in his heart. In the end, he had written her a simple love letter. A small investment for a very important message.

When Nick pulled up in front of Emmett's home, Holly's empty van was parked out front. Emmett answered the door, looking regal in a black velvet robe with red piping.

"Nick, I can't believe it's been a week," the older man commented, squinting against the sunlight. "Come on in. Holly's in the living room, and I was about to go upstairs to find out what's keeping Delilah when you knocked. I'll be back in a minute."

Nick watched Emmett climb the stairs before he let his gaze wander to the living room. Holly was standing beside the withered tree, watching him with a solemn expression.

"Good morning, Nick." Her tone was warm but not effusive. "I see Emmett called you, too."

"About an hour ago. I guess they're ready to see us again. How have you been?" He felt strained, overly polite.

She looked down at the carpet. "I'll be honest. I've missed you."

"If I said that I'd missed you, Holly, it would be an understatement." He stepped closer, longing to touch her cheek, to share her warmth. "You look so damn beautiful right now with your hair shining like copper in the sunlight and your soft gray eyes, haunting gray eyes. Why don't we just forget everything that's hanging between us, drive to the coast and go back to that bed-and-breakfast place in Astoria where we stayed in January?"

"Nick—"

"I'm talking about tomorrow morning after we spend this afternoon and tonight together making up for the days we've spent apart."

She shook her head and laughed.

"Forgive me, Holly. I'm an incurable romantic."

"I know and I hope they never find the cure." Holly cast a furtive glance at the stairway. "About Emmett and Delilah, should we treat them like friends or lovers? I don't want to make any assumptions and I don't want to belittle Delilah's marriage by implying—"

"Don't worry." Nick cleared his throat. "The private investigator said Clarence turned out to be a womanizer and a skunk. Delilah filed for a legal separation, and they lived apart for more than ten years before he died."

"That's sad, Nick."

"It gets worse. You know how Emmett said Clarence had no talent. He was right. The guy couldn't dance. After they moved to Hollywood, he wasn't able to get work in the movies."

"So maybe Emmett's gloating—no, he loves her. I have to believe that, Nick. He must be trying to make up for all the hurt she's gone through."

Seconds later, there were footsteps on the stairs and Delilah made a sweeping entrance, followed by Emmett.

"Beautiful day, isn't it?" Delilah hugged Holly and Nick. "It's so good to see you. I think Emmett has something he wants to say."

Emmett looked down at the floor for a moment, then up at Holly and Nick. "I called the two of you this morning because I wanted to tell you that Delilah will be going back to California very soon."

Holly felt a hollow ache in her chest. "I hope you'll remain friends. I'm just sorry things didn't work out."

"Well, there's the rest of the news." Emmett opened his arm out, and Delilah moved to his side. "I'll be going to California with her. We're getting married and she wants her kids to be there to see it."

"Thank God," Nick sighed. "We weren't sure whether to treat you like friends or lovers when we walked in here."

"We're both," Emmett said firmly. "We've wiped away the years. Only friends can do that. My one regret is that the two of you can't seem to agree on what you want—"

Emmett paused in mid-sentence and stood transfixed, staring at the top of the tree. "The star is gone!"

Nick turned and looked up at the pitiful remnant of a tree. "Holly?"

"Do you know what day this is?" she asked him, smiling.

"The last day of February." The realization dawned on him. "The end of our written commitment to Emmett, but it doesn't really have to end, Holly."

"No, it doesn't, but we probably won't see much of each other. Emmett and Delilah will be on their honeymoon—and we'll be on ours."

"You mean?"

"It's time to take the tree down, Nick. You were right." She reached into her jacket and brought out the star of tinsel. "I got your letter, Nick. I was happy because you chose to express yourself without flowers or extravagant gifts.

"And because everything you said was true." She ran her fingers over the shimmering surface of the star as she paused. "It can't be Christmas forever and we wouldn't want it to be. There's the first day of spring and the last day of summer, the harvest moon and a myriad of other reasons to celebrate special days throughout the year. They can all hold the same holiday magic I've been looking for all my life, and they will, Nick—because I love you."

She placed the star in his upturned palm as tears spilled onto her cheeks.

"Sretna Nova Godina," he whispered.

"You'll have to translate that for me," Holly said softly, her lips brushing the side of his mouth. "It might take me years to learn Croatian."

"It means Happy New Year, Holly, but it could mean new month, new day, new beginnings for all I care. I intend to share them all with you, love. Forever."

* * * * *

"Barbara Delinsky has a butterfly's touch for nuance that brings an exquisite sheen to her work."
—*Romantic Times*

Finger Prints

A nightmare begins for a young woman when she testifies in an arson trial. Fearing for her life, she assumes a new identity... only to risk it all for love and passion after meeting a handsome lawyer.

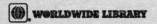

Silhouette Desire

1989
IS THE YEAR
OF THE MAN!

What makes a romance? A special man, of course, and Silhouette Desire celebrates that fact with *twelve* of them! From Mr. January to Mr. December, every month spotlights the Silhouette Desire hero—our **MAN OF THE MONTH.**

Sexy, macho, charming, irritating...irresistible! Nothing can stop these men from sweeping you away. Created by some of your favorite authors, each man is custom-made for pleasure—*reading* pleasure— so don't miss a single one.

Diana Palmer kicks off the new year, and you can look forward to magnificent men from **Joan Hohl, Jennifer Greene** and many, many more. So get out there and find your man!

Silhouette Desire's

MAN OF THE MONTH...

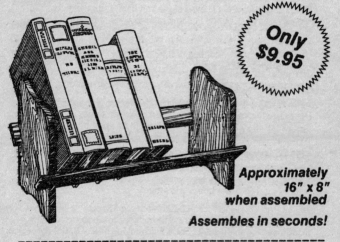

Silhouette Desire

COMING NEXT MONTH

#469 RELUCTANT FATHER—Diana Palmer
Meet our JANUARY MAN-OF-THE-MONTH, Blake Donavan. Tough. Formidable. He lived alone and liked it that way. His nemesis was love, but he had one obsession—her name was Meredith Calhoun.

#470 MONTANA'S TREASURES—Janet Bieber
G.T. Maddox loved his land too much to let Amanda Lukenas destroy it. He figured he'd offer some old-fashioned hospitality featuring his own special brand of . . . friendly persuasion.

#471 THAT FONTAINE WOMAN!—Helen R. Myers
District Attorney Adam Rhodes didn't like Fontaines and Diana was no exception. She was the kind of woman he knew he could never control, but one he ached to possess.

#472 HEARTLAND—Sherryl Woods
Friends. Steven Drake and Lara Danvers had once been much more than that. Now Steven had come back and he wanted Lara *and* her farm. Could she trust him . . . this time?

#473 TWILIGHT OVER EDEN—Nicole Monet
Amber Stevenson had to betray the man she loved to protect him from scandal and disgrace. She still loved Joe Morrow, but the secrets remained along with her passion.

#474 THIN ICE—Dixie Browning
Maggie Duncan had left a high-powered job and a failed marriage for her grandfather's cabin. She'd found peace in her solitude—but that was before Sam Canady arrived!
